Fly

M.A. McNally

Copyright © 2025 by M.A. McNally

All rights reserved.

No part of this book may be reproduced or transmitted by any means, electronic, mechanical, photocopying, or otherwise, without the prior permission of the author.

The moral right of the author has been asserted.

This is a work of fiction. Unless otherwise indicated, all the names, characters, businesses, places, events, and incidents in this book are either the product of the authors imagination or used in a fictitious manner. Any resemblance to actual person's, living or dead, or actual events, is purely coincidental.

Editor: - Sian Phillips – Proofreading services

Cover artist: Cameron McNally

Formatting by Romie Nguyen

Also by M.A. McNally

The Broken series

Book one, *Broken*

Book two, *Secrets*

Book three, *Truths*

Book four, *Fly*

To the memory of my darling friend, Kay, who sadly passed just before I published, and for my family, Andy, Charley, Heidi, Cameron, Steven, Max and Neil for their love and support.
I love you all.

CONTENT GUIDANCE:

This novel explores aspects of domestic abuse and mental health and contains depictions of self-harm, alcohol abuse, animal cruelty, blood and gore, child abuse. Please read with care.

Chapter One
Jesse

Unless you learn to FACE YOUR OWN SHADOWS, you will continue to see them IN OTHERS, because the WORLD OUTSIDE YOU, is only a REFLECTION of the WORLD INSIDE YOU.

— Unknown

12th January 1996 – Age Nineteen

"I've never told you this, but I think my father might be gay."

"What the hell? Where in God's name did that come from? You're such a crazy bitch. Why would you say that?"

"My father likes lots of musicals, loves decorating, and don't even get me started on his fashion sense. I've thought he was gay for ages. I haven't told a soul. It won't surprise me if he comes out one day. I mean, he's never openly fancied any women in front of me, like ever!"

That's the last proper conversation I remember having with my best friend, Lola. It seems a lifetime ago that we were sitting on the floor of her little flat above the pizza shop talking about random shit like that. We'd chatted about everything that night; I'd even opened up to her about my childhood and the night my mother flung me out of home, which happened to be the same night as her sixteenth birthday. I was only weeks away from being sixteen myself.

That night changed my life.

I hadn't known where I was going or what I was going to do, but the terror of being alone, cold, and moneyless with nothing but a bag and my beautiful cat, Samantha, is something I will remember for the rest of my life. Thank God I had Samantha.

Everything that happened that night I blame my mother for. I wouldn't have been chucked out like an old rag if her pervert friend, Kevin, hadn't been caught touching me up. He'd been doing it for months after she'd invited him over to the house after bumping into him on a rare day out. If she hadn't bumped into him, then I'd probably still be living at home, which means Jayden and I would never have met. But, God, the Devil, who knows, had other plans for me. When Kevin had visited that first Tuesday night I knew something wasn't right. I'd hoped that would be the last of him, but no, my stupid mother had started letting him visit every Tuesday night as long as he'd bought her thirty pieces of silver, her precious bottle of whisky.

The very first night he'd come, his filthy eyes had let me know loud and clear that he had no intention of reigniting any friendship with my mother. Those beady bullets had smiled; I'd frozen in fear as soon as they'd penetrated my skin. I'm sure he'd thought he'd struck gold. He'd definitely taken full advantage of the fact that my mother was mad, single, and an alcoholic.

The night I was thrown out, she'd awoken from her drunken sleep and had somehow stumbled out to the shed where she'd found his disgusting hands all over me.

Such a predator, he'd ambushed me too many times while she'd slept. He'd terrified me, turned me to stone and played with me as he'd pleased.

His hands were the devil.

Fly

When she'd found us, she'd actually accused me of 'seducing' him. Like I would ever have done that? She'd believed *him* and had thrown me out with only a bag, a flimsy coat, and my Samantha.

I will never forget that night for as long as I live.

I hope she's dead.

I hope that filthy, dirty, pervert, is dead too, or in prison. That'd be the karma he deserves.

I always knew my mother was mad, but her insanity reached new heights that night.

The funny thing is, I'd go back there in a heartbeat; go through that all over again if it meant escaping from the hell I'm in now.

Anywhere is better than here.

The night I'd opened up to Lola around at her flat, she'd been shocked by what I'd told her. She'd been shocked about a lot.

I can still see us sitting on the floor, talking, drinking, me telling her everything. It'd been so hard for her to imagine having to fend for herself in the big wide world. She'd been such a pampered princess. I would've paid money to have seen what she'd done in my position. I know that's cruel, but she wouldn't have lasted two minutes, let alone two years. She's lucky. Always has been. Her parents, however fucked up they are, love her to the moon and back. Well, maybe her dad does. I'm not so sure about her mother. Lola hates her, and has perpetually felt unloved by her most of her life. I've never met her mother, so I don't know if that's true or not. Some of the things Lola's told me about her though, aren't nice. She adores her dad, which is why I remember her saying she thought he was gay.

I don't know why her saying that is something that particularly stands out. We'd talked about so much more that night. I suppose it's because it was such a random thing to say in the middle of a conversation. I mean, we hadn't even been talking about it. It still makes me laugh.

The connection we'd had that night is something I'll treasure.

Of course, we probably won't ever talk like that again, because we no longer see each other. Jayden made sure of that.

I think about my old life a lot.

It's usually when I have hours to kill waiting for him to get home. Like now, for instance. He's been out all day doing God knows what.

He's such an arsehole.

Glancing at the clock, it's nearly three o'clock, which means he'll be back any minute.

Please let him have died in a freak crash.

Please, God, anyone, send him away.

If I could go back in time, I'd go straight back to that night around Lola's flat, talking about random shit.

I'd go back to the night I met Jayden and tell myself to not even look in his direction. I'd tell myself to run the fuck away.

Lola once told me she was going to find me someone to love.

"I'm determined to find you a bloody boyfriend by the end of the year. You deserve it after everything you've been through with your mother and the pervert. You deserve someone to love you, Jesse. He's out there. He's out there somewhere."

If only she knew.

The man I've ended up with doesn't love me, and certainly doesn't think I deserve to be loved. Lola had actually been jealous of the attention Jayden had given me that first time I'd seen him. I actually think she'd wanted him to like her, furious that he'd chosen me over her.

I bet she's ecstatic he didn't choose her, now.

I bet she thinks she dodged a bullet, and is thanking God that I ended up with him and not her.

Like I haven't been through enough crap throughout my life?

I don't bother trying to dodge his fists anymore. It wouldn't do any good anyway. Nothing I do is ever good enough, and everything I do pisses him off. It's like living in an active minefield every day not knowing if I'll step on a bomb and it'll kill me.

I'm not going to lie. Sometimes I really do wish he'd finish me off.

Lola wasn't happy when I started going out with him. Neither was my boss, Sharon, or Celeste, a friend from work, or Greg the DJ, or Joni, the bouncer at my favourite club. No one was, or I imagine, still is happy I'm with him. Me the most.

I'd do anything to be at Lola's again, telling me she thinks her dad's gay.

I miss those days - so - fucking - much.

Republica's 'Into the Darkness' plays in the background, tapping my finger in time to the beat, staring at my eyes through the mirror. Every time I hear this song I think the same thing. I love the beat, but the lyrics are crap. They're depressing and remind me too much about my life and how shit it is. I don't want reminding from anyone, especially the lovely Saffron, how shitty my life has ended up.

Staring at my rainbow eye, I hate to admit, it looks quite pretty with its different shades of purple, yellow, and green all blending together. The bruises have almost become like make-up to me, feeling semi naked without them. Stupid I know, to think that way, but I've got to find something to like about them otherwise I'll go fucking crazy.

Massaging the skin around my right eye with my fingers, I'm amazed it feels so soft, and I'm amazed it's nearly back to normal after the beating Jayden gave me six weeks ago. I thought I'd die that night and had freaked out a few days later when my eye had opened and I'd seen the inside was completely red. I thought it might stay that way forever, had covered it up for weeks with sunglasses just so I wouldn't scare any more kids when Jayden had actually allowed me to go for a walk with him.

Thank God it's nearly back to normal but the bone above my eye droops a bit now.

Jayden, the prick, hasn't even noticed.

When I met him, I really thought he would change my life. God knows I'd needed it changing after spending years with the world's most abusive mother. I'd watched the old bitch drink and smoke herself to oblivion most nights, even emptied her bucket of pee she kept beside her bed because she couldn't be arsed to get up and go to the toilet like everyone else. I'm sure the only pleasure in life she got was tormenting me daily with shit like that.

You'd think God had punished me enough giving me her for a mother, but no, He went and let the bitch add Kevin to the mix. He never penetrated me, thank God, but the things he made me do to him, I'll never forget. His hands loved my breasts, and had made my last six months at home worse than anything my mother had ever done to me. I'd prayed a miracle would happen and he'd die, or I'd sleep right through to Wednesday, but it'd never happened.

I hate remembering what he used to make me do, but I'm reminded of it every time Jayden touches me because he uses my body worse than Kevin ever did.

He uses me like a piece of meat.

I can't forget, even if I want to.

The night Samantha and I were thrown out with just a bag of clothes and a flimsy coat, Kevin was there. I was so terrified; I still can't believe I made it all the way to the city in one piece. That first night in a park, huddled under a box, was one of the worst nights of my life. I thought Samantha and I would definitely be killed but, by some miracle, I met a woman the very next morning who saved my life. I was supposed to meet her, of that I'm sure.

Gail saved me in more ways than one. For one, Samantha would be dead. She saved her from crossing a very busy road and being killed. I don't know what I would've done if that had happened. Gail was so lovely. She took me by the hand and walked me to a café she knew to calm me down; before I knew it, she was moving Samantha and I into her place. She, unbeknown to me, was the queen of the streets that no-one messed with. Not even the pimps!

Gail showed me what love was. I had never been loved so much in my life than when I was with her.

I was only with her a short time, but she ended up teaching me the ropes. After about two weeks, Gail asked her best friend, Sharon, to give me a job. That's how I ended up at The Orchard. Sharon

Fly

owned it. I knew it was a brothel, but I didn't care. Anywhere was better than where I grew up.

I worked there for nearly two years, until recently.

I miss Sharon so much.

I miss the girls.

I miss my old life.

I miss everything.

I didn't know at the time, but the morning after I was given that job would be the saddest day of my life.

It's still hard for me to think about it. I found Gail ... dead.

She'd had a massive heart attack in the night and died, just like that.

Nothing prepares you for that much sadness. I loved her more than anything, thought of her as the mother I always wanted. What made it worse, was that I'd found out the night before that we were *related*. It still blows my mind that Gail was my mother's *sister*. I didn't even know my mother had family.

Placing my hands on my necklace around my neck, I kiss the centre, remembering my aunt. I wish she could've stayed alive for just a bit longer.

Studying the necklace through the mirror, I still remember when Gail had handed it to me. It was the night before she died and we'd been having a few celebratory drinks for me getting the job at The Orchard. The necklace is how we figured out she and my mother were sisters. I'd seen the exact replica of it for years hanging over one of my mother's pictures in her bedroom. I'd wanted to steal it so many times.

Rubbing the centre, bringing it to my lips, I can still see Gail giving it to me, making me promise to reunite it with her daughter. Gail had twins, two girls, one born on a toilet floor in a train station, the other left at the hospital. I couldn't believe what she was telling me.

I've actually got *cousins* out there somewhere.

The one she'd given birth to on the toilet floor was apparently taken by a woman who'd helped her give birth. The Angel Lady is all Gail knew her by.

It was so hard for me to believe she'd just let some random woman take her baby, but nothing really surprised me about Gail. She had more stories than you could throw a stick at.

Gail's second baby was born in hospital. She left an identical necklace in her cot with a note she'd hand written before she'd slipped out for a cigarette and never returned.

The baby was only a week old.

Gail told me she wore her necklace every day after leaving her second daughter at the hospital. She told me she'd had two identical necklaces; one she'd stolen from her mother, which is the one she wore, and the one she'd left at the hospital with her second daughter.

The bump in the middle of the necklace is so smooth between my fingers, still not believing I'm wearing my grandmother's necklace. Gail told me her mother, like mine, was a monster. Perhaps that's why she died so suddenly? I think finding out her sister was just as much a monster as their mother would've killed her.

My necklace was supposed to have been given to her first daughter, the one she'd given birth to on the floor of the train station toilet. In all the chaos Gail said she hadn't remembered to give it to her. She'd made me promise to find her second daughter and give it to her, which of course, I did, but I knew it would be near enough impossible.

Finding out Gail and my mother were related was like a grenade going off in my hand. My head was ready to explode with so much new information. I'd never even known my mother had family, let alone a *sister*. I remember feeling happy and sad at the same time. Happy because I'd always wanted an aunty, and sad because I hadn't known her forever.

I'll never forget the day Gail died. *Ever*.

The numbness came back.

I started cutting myself again.

Sharon, bless her, took me in.

Fly

The Orchard became my home and for nearly two years I worked there, made friends, and life became happier. Sharon took over from Gail and became my mother figure.

I love Sharon to the moon and back and would do anything for her especially as she saved me from *Kevin* when he'd unexpectedly turned up at The Orchard one night. If it weren't for Sharon, I don't know what would have happened.

I don't know why, but after I saw him, I thought about Zoe, my best friend who I hadn't seen for nearly two years. It was close to her eighteenth birthday, so on a whim I'd decided to get on a train and go and surprise her. I needed some sort of normality back in my life and, if I'm honest, I missed her even though she was a bitch for most of my life growing up. I didn't care. She would've definitely known exactly what to do if she'd seen Kevin. I needed that comfort. I needed her. I had a great job, and some lovely friends, but I still didn't really know how to look after myself, and, I suppose, I knew Zoe would look after me. She'd always done from primary school right through secondary school, up until the night I'd been flung out of home.

We'd reunited and it was just like old times. When she'd moved to the city to be near me, I thought my life couldn't get any better.

Almost immediately she'd changed her name to Lola, apparently to piss her mother off. She'd hated her mother with as much passion as I'd hated mine. I've never really understood why. It's not as though her life was ever *that* bad.

Thinking about the time she told me her father was gay, I'd do anything to be there again, laughing, listening to music, smoking a joint like we used to. I haven't seen or talked to her in so long. I stopped seeing her soon after Jayden came onto the scene.

He wanted that to happen.

He wanted me all to himself.

Everyone's gone.

All I have left is, Samantha.

I miss Lola.

I miss Gail.

I miss Sharon.

I miss them so much.

Bringing my necklace to my lips, it's coldness comforts me, remembering Gail. If I could go back in time to the day I met her, I'd change so much. I'd change everything.

I've asked myself a million times why I'm still here, with Jayden, in his locked flat, looking into a stupid mirror, getting ready for one of *his* sordid fantasies - again. If a friend of mine was in the exact same position, I'd be telling her to run the fuck away, so why aren't I?

Why aren't I?

I constantly feel numb, except for when I'm being beaten, or cutting myself, or feeling scared, which is ninety-nine percent of the time.

I feel crazy.

I always feel crazy.

Stupidly, I thought Jayden was *the one*. When I met him at DevO's, my favourite nightclub, I thought he was my knight in shining armour, sent to rescue me from my nightmares of my bitch mother and Kevin. I would've done anything to get away from the memories of them. I'd fantasised for so long about meeting someone who'd sweep me off my feet and take me away from it all. When Jayden had asked me out, I hadn't thought twice. I'd jumped without looking where I was going.

It backfired big time.

I didn't think for one minute he'd turn out to be a million times worse than my mother and the pervert combined.

I was so blinded by the fantasy of what I wanted.

I was so blinded, I couldn't see what was right in front of me.

If I could go back and live with my mother again, I would. Living with that monster was a whole lot better than the one I'm living with, now.

I can't believe I'm even saying that!

Fly

If I could, I'd break out of this stupid flat, fly away somewhere far, far away, with Samantha, and be happy.

I'd fly to England, a place I've always wanted to go.

I'd fly to the moon and never come back.

But, it's impossible. I can't go anywhere. I'm trapped in this second floor flat with two locks on the front door, and there is nothing I can do but look out the windows. I've tried to unpick the locks, even resorted to banging them with a hammer, but the neighbours heard and told Jayden so I've never done it again. That hadn't ended well.

Lighting another joint, the smell is strong, like sweet grass burning. Jayden only gets the best weed, so at least I know I'll enjoy it.

Laying back in the chair, blowing smoke out my nose, the scissors on my dresser catch my eye, the blades grabbing the sun coming through my window. Snatching them, still puffing on my smoke, I feel the blades sharpness on my finger, quickly removing my smoke, sucking my finger, tasting my blood as it mixes with the nicotine. I can't say I like the taste, but it doesn't make me baulk anymore having tasted it a thousand times since I met Jayden. Sucking the end of my joint like a hoover, I hover the blade over the top of my left arm, the fumes from my nose dancing around it like an exotic smoky temptress.

Should I do it?

Should I cut myself before the prick gets home?

Placing my joint in the overflowing ashtray, watching through the mirror, the top of my arm turns deep red waiting for the burn, my heart jumping around my chest like popcorn hitting the top of a lid.

Burning. Exhilarated, the numbness flies away.

Running down my arm; blood lands on my tight white PVC nurse's outfit, quickly licking my finger and washing it away. If Jayden sees it, I may as well punch myself and be done with it.

I look so stupid, so false. I never wear pigtails, or make-up this thick. I have to wear thick make-up to cover up the bruises because if Jayden sees them, he'll punch me. He never likes to see what he's done.

Ignoring my blood, quickly covering my rainbow eye with as much concealer as I can, I touch up my dark eyeliner and make sure my lips are overdone with gloss. If I don't look even remotely close to the women in the videos Jayden watches, I don't even want to think about what he'll do.

Don't get me wrong. I *hate* those women and *don't* want to look like them. Who would? But not being punched is way more important to me at the moment than worrying about looking like a whore. I've often thought what it would be like for all the blood to leave my body. But the thought of leaving Samantha here alone with Jayden stops me.

I can't die, not yet.

While she is alive, I have to protect her. I'm sure Jayden wants to kill her. He doesn't pretend to like her one little bit. In fact, I've seen his eyes follow her, like a lion hunting its prey and it scares me shitless. Samantha hates him, which I have to take notice of. I know she's just a cat, but the bond we have is untouchable. We know what each other is feeling; I have to protect my baby. She is my world, my reason for still being here, so I'm sure as hell not going to let anything happen to her while I'm still alive to protect her.

I've often wondered why Jayden is so violent, so cruel. It's bad enough he hurts me, but if he ever hurt her, I don't know what I'd do. I'd probably try and kill him. Deep down, I know I'd be the one who comes out dead. If Samantha was dead, I'd be dead, too. She deserves to be protected from his cruel hands. She's just an animal and has no choice.

I bought her an old, pink, brocade coat from a charity shop when I first moved into The Orchard to put in her basket. I don't know why I was so drawn to it. I remember trying it on in the shop just for fun and thinking how on earth anyone could wear it. You'd need to be super strong to wear it all day. Looking across to the coat now covered in silver hair, the heaviness I remember feeling is all too present living here, with Jayden. It feels like I'm wearing that brocade coat over me every hour of every minute of every day.

Fly

That's why I cut.

Everything feels lighter when I cut.

I wish all the time I'd never laid eyes on Jayden. I especially think about it after a beating. I fantasise about my life and how different it would've been if I'd met someone else.

I make up all sorts of stories in my head, convincing myself the fairy-tale I want so much to come true will happen, soon, and someone new will come and rescue me.

Isn't that what's supposed to happen? Boy meets girl, rescues her from her crappy fucked-up world, and they live happily ever after. Not, girl meets boy, who tricks her into thinking he loves her and before it's too late, she's living with him, and every penny she's saved has been fleeced off her. Not only that, he controls everything she does, traps her in a flat, beats her up and makes her do fucked-up things for the rest of her life.

Fairy tales really are screwed up. They aren't real. Little girls and boys need to know they've been led up the garden path by the adults in their lives who make them read stupid stories, or watch stupid films about being rescued by a prince and they think it's real. Not that my mother or any other adult led me up any garden path. If my mother had read me a story, or had watched even one film that hadn't had an abnormal amount of devil worship, violence, or sex in it, that would've been a miracle. I would've felt she cared just a little bit.

It wasn't her who led me up the garden path. *I* did that myself. I read all those stories, and watched those stupid films, believing they could possibly be true. The thought of it was so romantic.

Of course, I've found out the hard way that those stories are the fakest of fake. I need to tell people the truth, especially all the girls like me before they make the same dumb mistakes. I need to tell them before they make the same mistakes as hundreds of thousands of people out there falling for the same monsters who disguise themselves in false smiles and false charm. The monsters who make you believe they love you, absolutely positive they have feelers on their heads with radars that search out all the women, men, girls, boys, people who haven't been loved. The ones who are desperate to be rescued.

I know because I was one of them.

Still am.

I want to scream, tell everyone like me not to fall for it. I want to tell them to *run the fuck away*.

I should've trusted myself. I should've listened to my gut. But I didn't. I didn't run the hell away, and look where I am now?

Looking into the mirror, cutting myself again, a lone sock next to the ashtray has specks of blood on it, picking it up and cleaning the blades with it.

Sitting, staring at my reflection, I think of my old life and how I still have nightmares about it. Now, I hate to admit, Jayden has joined them, too.

Sometimes, when I wake in the middle of the night and see the perverts face above me, Jayden's there, with him. I lay in bed, unable to move anything but my eyes, praying there are no hands all over me. I breathe in and out, looking around to see if I'm back at home, relieved when I see I'm in the flat. But then I start panicking all over again because I'm not alone. Jayden's lying right beside me. I try not to disturb him because I know what will happen if he wakes. He'll start touching me; I always feel dirty when he touches me. It's like a skunk's scent that won't rub off. God knows I've scrubbed my skin over and over and over, but it's never any use. I still smell him on me and I hate it.

When I wake, I look over to him and imagine I'm *Wonder Woman*, a strong, single-minded slayer ready to rid the world of another monster. I imagine smothering Jayden with my pillow, me on top of him as he struggles, pushing the pillow harder into his face until he can't struggle anymore. When I think he's dead, I lift the pillow, smiling, happy that he's no longer able to breathe, and the bastard is always there, smirking up at me before his hands pounce on my throat.

I hate him.

Fly

I hate him so - bloody - much.

If I had the guts to kill him, my nightmare would be over, but I'm not a psycho, like him. I know the difference between right and wrong, and anyway, my conscience wouldn't live with it.

It's a fantasy.

I just wish I could go through with it.

If he woke up and found me with a pillow over his head, I don't like to think what would happen to me. He'd definitely kill me, but before he did, I'm sure the prick would tie me up and make me watch while he tortured my Samantha; the only reason I tell myself not to do it. I can't let that happen. Ever. I can't ever see my baby hurt, especially by *him*! I have to stay alive to protect her. She is my safety blanket, my life.

I remember back to when the pervert had her in his hand, hovering her above my head as she snarled and hissed at him. I protected her from evil hands then, and I'll protect her from evil hands, now. I've asked myself over and over if I'm with an even worse version of the pervert. I didn't think you could get eviller than that.

In the beginning I thought the stars had aligned and Jayden and I had been pulled together by some great unknown force. I had still hoped my fairy tale would come true.

I learned pretty fast that the only thing on his mind back then, and now, is the one thing I truly despise.

Sex.

I wasn't chosen above all the other women out there because I was special. No one is special in Jayden's eyes, but himself. He doesn't know how to love, and even though I haven't been lucky enough to have been loved throughout my life, I know I'd feel it if someone did. Surely. What Jayden does isn't love. What Jayden loves is control. He could've chosen anyone, even an animal, so why was I the unlucky one he chose?

I think about that all the time.

In my head I know what he is doing is wrong, but I hate myself, and don't think anyone else will want me, so I figure it's better to put up with all of Jayden's crap than be alone. Isn't it? Some days I want to run as far away as I can get, and other days all I want to do is ignore the world and curl up in my bed with Samantha and sleep. I'm exhausted from it all, can't think straight. I feel like I'm going crazy.

When Jayden and I first met, there were a few gorgeous dates and it didn't take long for us to move to the bedroom. Even though I'd been molested by Kevin, I was still a virgin, and didn't know the first thing about meaningful sex. I knew I didn't want to just give anything away. My virginity was something I cherished, especially after everything the pervert had done, so the decision to give myself to Jayden was huge.

That first time had been nothing but wonderful. I'd felt so connected, so wanted by someone, finally. We'd talked for hours about what we liked, didn't like, our favourite food, music. Of course I could only go out with him on a Wednesday, my day off, so we'd spent the whole day and night together, ecstatic to be with someone who I felt really wanted to be with me. The first month had been blissful. It actually felt like I was floating on a cloud, so light that any thought of my old life was non-existent. I didn't think love could be that good.

After the first month of dates, the thought of losing him had made me feel sick. No one had ever wanted me like that. *Ever*. I'd always been invisible to men in that way, until him. I'd never been given a second glance over Lola. She was gorgeous, perfect in fact. Men had never looked at me with the same lust, except Greg, the DJ at DevO's, the nightclub we went to, but he didn't count.

Jayden had totally ignored Lola, and chosen *me*. That in itself was a miracle I couldn't ignore. Looking back, it's so obvious. He reeled me in like a fish that didn't know what it was eating. You see, back then the bait was far too delicious for me to ignore.

His attention. His lust. His interest.

For once someone had wanted *me*.

Fly

I'd lapped it all up like a puppy because I was too delirious, intoxicated with what was happening.

Fast forward nearly two years, and here I am, sitting in front of a mirror, cutting myself again because Jayden is able to pull me backwards and forwards like a piece of elastic. Loving me, pushing me away, begging me to come back, pulling away again and again, leaving me distraught, panicky that I'm unable to think of life without him. One day I'll snap, and then what will happen.

Why haven't I snapped yet?

Every thought, day and night, revolves around *him*.

All the people I love have gone because I've abandoned them all to be with him. I'd do anything to have them back. I'd do anything to go back in time and start again.

All I have left is Samantha.

Feeling her rubbing my legs under the dressing table, I pick her up and softly stroke her, pressing her cheek to mine through the mirror, hugging her with more force than she wants. Meowing, she jumps off.

"Don't leave me, baby. Come back."

Meowing again, she walks off to another room with blood on her fur; I turn, facing the mirror, watching the blood continuing to run down my arm. Ignoring it, I grab my joint out of the ashtray and light it, inhaling, as I trace around my right eye with my finger.

I remember how the beatings started.

It was a simple slap across my cheek. Six months almost to the day after I met Jayden. Just a simple slap. How could I have been so fucking stupid, so blind ...

Chapter Two

Don't be blinded by love.

— Unknown

November 27th 1994 – Age Eighteen

Where the hell is Jayden? He said he'd be back straight after the film to take me out for a something to eat. I'm bloody starving. I need to pee, too. Doesn't he know it's nearly eleven o'clock? *Once Were Warriors* must've been longer than he thought.

Bladder bursting, I can't wait any longer for him to get home. I'll bloody explode before that. Why the hell he tells me not to leave the room until he's back, it's like I'm a child. What does he think I'm going to do? I'm on my own, in a tiny room, in a rented house, and on top of that, I have to use the shared bathroom across the hall, which grosses me out.

Unlocking the bedroom door, focusing every muscle on trying not to pee myself, I know how much trouble I'll get into if Jayden comes home now, but I have to take the risk. I can't wait. Locking the door quickly behind me and running to the shared bathroom across the hall, a tiny trickle of urine escapes.

The wooden door creaks, closing it, freezing on the spot as a filthy-looking man standing outside a room opposite, watches me intently, nearly peeing myself in fright. He must've come from nowhere because twenty seconds ago there was no-one but me on the landing. He looks familiar, sure I've seen him and his scruffy face somewhere before, but I'm not sure where. What the hell is he doing here this late? I know everyone who lives in this house, and he definitely doesn't.

Unfreezing myself and slamming the door and locking it, my jeans fight to unzip, crossing my legs, finally landing on the toilet with a thud. Closing my eyes, smiling up to the ceiling, I hum the first song that comes into my head, my bladder sighing with relief as it's emptied.

In the blink of an eye it all goes wrong.

I can't move.

My worst nightmare.

Staring up at eight huge hairy legs crawling above me, the black hairy face is daring me to make any noise. I *hate* spiders, I *hate* this stupid shared house, and I *hate* being here, in this stupid shared toilet which I'm not allowed to go to on my own unless Jayden's home. It's so fucked up.

Our bedroom is so small; there's not any room to move let alone live in it. I begged Jayden to leave the key in case of a fire, and he finally gave in, but I had to agree to pee in the sink in our room if I was really bursting. I can't even *fit* in the sink, it's *so* small. We drink out of that sink! I made sure to keep my fingers crossed behind my back when I agreed to it. Thank God Jayden never saw me.

If he comes home now and finds I've used the key for anything other than a fire, he'll kill me. He's promised he'll never hit me, but I don't believe him. He gets angry too quickly, and there's a scary look in his eyes when he does. It's like it's not really him. I don't like the way he watches me, especially when we're watching television.

He watches everything.

"I saw you looking at that guy. Do you think he's sexy? Do you like him, then?"

I never answer.

Jumping up from the toilet, not bothering to wipe myself, my jeans stick like glue to my now sweaty legs, trying to pull them up while I keep my eyes on the hairy beast crawling across the ceiling into a slit in the wall. Squealing like a pig, this is the last thing I need.

Still looking up, making sure the ugly eight-legged freak has gone, I wash and dry my hands, looking into the mirror, noticing how much weight is dropping off my face. I've not even been on a diet. It's probably from the amount of sex I'm having. Jayden's appetite for it is insatiable. He doesn't even give me a break when I'm on my period, saying he's heard sex helps with the pain.

It definitely doesn't.

Unlocking the bathroom door, the filthy man is still there, waiting outside the same room.

Should I just run for it?

Looking backwards and forwards from him to my room, they are metres apart. Keys at the ready, walking forward like I mean business, the filthy man starts moving towards me with a psycho smile; suddenly I'm a statue. Mind in slow motion, all at once, I'm not worried for my safety from him, but more from Jayden if he comes home now and sees me with him.

Quickly unfreezing myself, turning back and slamming the bathroom door, I lock it, stuck to the back of it, breathing like I've just run a marathon. Keys jingling, I don't know what to do. The adrenaline is making my head feel like it could float off my shoulders with all the thoughts racing around it, confused as the various concerns overlap each other.

What if the man stays outside all night.

What if he's still there when Jayden returns.

What will Jayden do to him. To me.

What if, what if, what if.

Fly

Turning, peering through the keyhole, I'm wide-awake, watching, waiting for him to leave, but he's pacing backwards and forwards, talking to himself, twitching, his eyes fixed on the door as if he can see right through it.

Can he?

Average height, he stops, fixated on the wood, dressed in a grimy, pale-green vest with Kermit the Frog on it, who smiles at me through rib bones so sharp, you'd swear he was a skeleton.

I knew I'd seen him before.

It was on a bus, on my way to my friend, Celeste's, house. How could I forget a vest like that? I'd stood underneath him and felt sick because he'd stunk so much. He probably stinks now; I don't really want to find out. Surely, he's cold. It's nearly midnight, and he's wearing next to nothing.

Why is he here? I hope he remembers I helped him, gave him money.

Staring at the bathroom door from where he stands, the dark hollows around his sunken eyes make him look like one of the living dead. Googly, frog-like eyes stare with pure malevolence at the door as grey, greasy, grubby sweatpants covered in white and red paint marks fall off his skeletal hips. I'm sure he was wearing those the last time I saw him. Walking backwards and forwards, his old white trainers with holes in both feet have rubber underneath coming away, flapping, keeping up with his incessant pacing. Unusually large feet poke out the top showing filthy toenails that blend in with his dirty shoes. A long, pale face with a scruffy tangled beard the same colour as his matted, dirty, off the shoulder blonde hair, suddenly stops again and stares at the door.

Without warning, he races towards me, and one eye as blue as the sky looks through the keyhole with an iris so dilated, I'm surprised he can see.

Jolting from the door, the smell of glue seeps through the keyhole making me want to be sick.

"What do you want? *Leave me alone.* My boyfriend will be home soon, you just wait."

Bang.

A foot kicks the door, making me jump back in fright. Thankfully, the door is made of solid wood, slumping to the floor at the same time the spider comes out of its slit and watches, like it's in cahoots with the maniac outside. Trapped from all angles, what am I going to do? All I can do is hope that someone comes to use the toilet soon so I can ask for help.

An hour later, staring at the lunatic through the keyhole until my eyes ache in their sockets, he's still pacing around on the landing, rubbing his hands together, looking at the door, laughing to himself.

My bladder's crying to be emptied again, risking it and quickly sitting on the toilet. Terrified, anxious, petrified of him, and even more of Jayden coming home, I look through the keyhole, clumsily zipping up my jeans, praying he leaves. Thanking God twenty seconds later, the lunatic shoots me through the keyhole with his fingers, winking, blowing me a kiss before finally walking off.

Grabbing my chance and running back to my room, my heart is pounding like a huge drum in my chest, watching, listening for any clue he might still be near. Key ready to insert into the lock, the door at the bottom of the stairs suddenly opens; looking towards the staircase, dropping my keys, quickly bending down, fumbling to pick them up while I watch the staircase in slow motion praying it isn't Jayden. Please don't let it be Jayden.

"No."

Frantically feeling for my keys, my fingertips aren't finding them, petrified of the psychotic grin metres away from me. Sweat dripping down my face, I don't want to die like this.

My keys. *Where the fuck are they?*

Scooping them up, I don't know how, but I find the right one, unlocking the door and entering, slamming it shut just before he gets to it.

Banging from behind, he's trying to get in, having to push hard against the door with my shoulder to stop him. He's much stronger than he looks.

Locking it from inside, sick with fear, I retch, peeing myself.

Tap, tap, tap.

Saying nothing, turning, peering through the keyhole, my body won't stop shaking. One piercing blue eye stares through it.

His high husky voice turns my body cold.

"Let me in, beautiful lady. You all alone? I'll protect you. I know you're in there. I been watching you. I know your boyfriend's not there. All I want is some money. That's all. Money. Give me some money. *Before I rip your skin off!*"

Thud, thud, thud.

Banging the door with his foot, something sharp scratches down the length of it. Is it a knife, a fingernail? I can't tell.

Where is Jayden? This wouldn't be happening if he'd just come home when he said he would. Other people live in this house. They rent rooms, so surely, they can hear what's going on. Why isn't anyone coming to help?

I don't know what to do.

I could run to Lola's flat when the lunatic leaves, but Jayden would kill me when I get back. I could tell him I thought there was a fire, and that's why I left.

I have to get out, away from this place, away from maniacs like the one outside my room.

Sliding down the door, nearly hitting Jayden's old brown battered box, I wrap my arms around my legs, swaying backwards and forwards, thinking of my old life at The Orchard. I'd do anything to hear '*Hong Kong Garden*' again.

Why did I leave. I felt so much safer there.

Humming the song in my head, rocking in time to the beat, something sharp hits me from underneath the door.

"Leave me alone. *Leave me alone!*"

Two and a half hours later, staring at Jayden's locked brown box, I'd love to know what's inside. Hearing movement outside, his key in the door signals he's finally home, scrambling to my feet as he lets himself in. Crying with relief to see him, I need a hug, wrapping my arms around his neck, him pushing me off, sniffing the air.

"Why the fuck were you on the floor in the dark with my box? Have you tried to open it? *Have you?*"

Why is he being so cold. I don't give a fuck about his stupid box. I need a hug, pulling him towards me again, but he pushes me off, sneering when he sees the wet patch between my legs.

"Have you pissed yourself? What the fuck."

Telling him what's happened, his bloodshot black eyes stare straight ahead, not blinking. I don't think he believes me, suddenly screaming, scaring me.

"*Why the fuck didn't you stay in the room like I told you? I told you to lock the door and wait for me, didn't I? Why didn't you piss in the sink? I fucking told you not to leave the room for anything unless there was a fire. Anything!*"

Slap.

Burning, numb, the side of my face vibrates from where his left-hand has whacked me hard across my cheek. My face stings, my ear sings, my nose burns. I have to get out.

"You bastard. You said you'd never hit me. *Ever.* Get out of my way. I was so scared."

Packing my bag, suddenly his eyes change and become softer. He's back to himself, speaking in a voice I recognise.

"No, baby. Please. I'm so sorry. It's just, I love you so much, I don't want anything to happen to you when I'm not here to protect you. Please. I promise, it won't happen again. Please. It was a mistake. A mistake. It'll never happen again. I promise."

Fly

Crying on my shoulder, begging for my forgiveness, he says it's a one off, a reaction to his fear of me being hurt.

"*Fuck off.* I don't believe you. Get out of my way. I'm going back to The Orchard."

Pulling me towards him, he cries on my shoulder begging me to give him one chance. I start to soften, feeling sorry for him. I can tell he's sorry for what he's done. He's crying, so he *must* feel bad. It's a one off for sure and won't happen again. I know it. No one has ever loved me this much. I'll give him one chance. I'm different from all the other girls ...

Chapter Three

I trusted you but now your words mean nothing to me, because your actions spoke the truth.

— *Unknown*

That first slap sealed my fate. Why the hell hadn't I run when I'd had the chance. Why the hell hadn't I listened to my gut.

Of course, it wasn't a one off. I stupidly believed him when he said he'd never do it again, his famous last words. That one slap turned into a slap every month, and after he moved to the flat I'm sitting in now, it quickly upped to a slap and punch every week. Very soon, all I felt were the cold tiles in the bathroom, the grainy wooden panels of the kitchen floor, and the concrete stairs outside the back door. I hadn't seen it coming, which is why I fell so hard.

To cope with it all, I started smoking more and more weed. I'd only ever had the odd puff with Lola, not surprised how soon I came to rely on it to make me feel better. I'd never experienced getting really high before. I felt lighter, less worried, and the sex was *amazing*. I'd actually let myself go, and for a tiny moment had forgotten about all the crap at home with my mother and the pervert.

Jayden used to be so gentle, so responsive to my needs. In the beginning I'd thought I was the luckiest girl in the world. His mouth had licked, kissed my body, and settled between my legs too many times to remember. I'd never felt so alive. I'd never felt so loved. I really thought it was going to be like that forever.

I was so stupid.

A year and a half down the line, just the sight of him makes me sick. I hate sex, and weed now makes me panic, unless I smoke it on my own.

When I smoke it with him, I'm convinced my heart is going to give way. I can't control how it beats. I can't control anything anymore, even my own panic. The need to control my breathing overpowers me, so I always end up letting Jayden distract me with sex, even though I know it's the last thing I want. My body responds to it, betrays me, so now I hate that, too, which is part of the reason I mutilate it.

Sex is as far away from my first experience as you could get.

Jayden tells me over and over no one will want me, love me as much as he does. He's probably right. His words are the things that make me stay.

I don't want him, but I'm too scared to leave. I'm too scared to be on my own. I'm scared of everything.

One day I will find the guts to go.

I will.

I don't mind admitting I've become comfortable with him hurting me. There's something familiar about it that makes it easy for me to handle in a way that it doesn't make me have to think too hard. I think it's because it reminds me of living with my mother and, I suppose, it's easier for me to feel unloved, than loved.

I *don't* want him, but I *don't* want anyone else to want him, either. I hate that he has such a hold over me and I've reasoned that if I put up with all his shit, and he suddenly changes into someone better, then why should somebody else get the better version of him. He's bound to change for me in time if I show him how much I'm willing to put up with, isn't he? I'm special, he's told me.

Jayden used to be gorgeous and kind, it wasn't bad all the time. His softer side was the one I fell in love with. The one I know still exists.

I used to help him cook, and we'd play music and sing along to songs while he played his guitar, which he's really good at. We'd make love like the first time we met, and then, just like that, I'd say something, or look at something or someone the wrong way, and it would change.

Now, I'm on guard from the moment my eyes open until they close, always watching my back, always watching where his eyes roam.

Not knowing if he'll kill me from one day to the next excites me in a warped way. I suppose it's a way of controlling something in my life. Whether I breathe or not is not actually his decision, it's mine.

Don't get me wrong, I know it's a dangerous game, but I can't seem to stop playing Russian roulette with my life. The constant pushing and pulling of his affections is something I need, crave, want, deserve.

Sometimes I think I'm as addicted to him as he is to his drugs, his porn, me.

Am I just the same?

Am I crazy?

If I am, at least I am in control of something, even if it is my life.

Still touching my right eye, tracing the outline of the bruising, I wonder, will today be the day I let him kill me.

Hearing his voice in my head, it all seems so transparent, now. Why didn't I see it? How could I have been so blind.

"Don't go out with Lola tonight."

"Are you really going to wear that?"

Fly

"I like you in clothes that don't show so much."
"I want you all to myself."
"I don't really want any man but me looking at you like that."
"I love you so much, baby. I'd die if you left me for anyone else."

I used to think his jealousy was flattering. I sort of got a buzz from someone wanting me so much. Now it's just tedious, predictable, soul destroying. All the people I love are gone, except Samantha. At least he let me keep her.

I've been bitten too many times now with his poison to leave. It's far too potent for me to escape its grasp, and, I think I'm as addicted to him as he is to me.

I remember when he used to turn up at my work uninvited. I'd thought nothing of it, ecstatic that he'd surprised me to come say hello, or take me to lunch.

Now I know it was because he didn't like me working at The Orchard. It's all so clear now. He came to spy on the men coming and going, and not to surprise me at all.

Sharon hated him the instant she met him, and the girls. They were stunned I even knew him. Apparently, Jayden was well known on the streets for taking drugs and being a creep. I didn't know any of it, and, if I'm honest, I didn't want to.

I didn't want anything to spoil what I had. I defended him, of course. Wouldn't anyone have defended the person they love?

Sharon, tired of his uninvited visits, eventually banned him from coming, saying he was scaring off customers with his filthy looks. After I explained to him he couldn't come anymore, his fists showed me how angry he was.

My friends started to distance themselves from me and eventually stopped talking to me. They talked to me at work, but that was to see what shifts they were on. Even Lola stopped talking to me and started asking for information about her shifts from Ramona, her arch enemy.

I knew things were bad when that started happening. She would never have talked to her.

Ever.

In the end I quit my job. But, to make doubly sure I never went back, I deliberately made sure Sharon found my hand in the till.

One of my lowest days.

I wish so much it was like it was in the beginning with Jayden, but it's not. I go from still being in love with him, to wanting to kill him, to wanting to kill myself. I don't know what I want anymore. The only two things I love and concentrate on now are Samantha and my music. My music has never let me down.

When I found out that Jayden loved music, too, I was beside myself with excitement. We'd bonded over songs, artists, and lyrics while I'd sat listening as he'd played his guitar to his favourite *Dire Straits* song. I'd tried to sing along, laughing when it was obvious I hadn't a clue what any of the words were, then afterwards we'd made love looking into each other's eyes, listening to *Minnie Riperton* singing, 'ced the first time his raised hand had come into contact with my face. That first slap had sealed my fate.

Meow.

Thank God I still have Samantha.

Gently patting more concealer onto the bruising around my right eye, humming '*Hey Jude,*' I'm still unsure why I even like the song. I shouldn't after what Jayden did to me.

I shouldn't be here.

Fly

I shouldn't be anywhere near him.

Feeling fur on my legs, the song, '*Hey Jude,*' surrounds me like a bubble, remembering back to the night I should've left Jayden. I should've packed my bags and run the fuck away and never looked back …

Chapter Four

I will never be the same. Never. He took something away from me, mentally and physically.

— *Valerie Aerni*

July 28th 1995—Age Nineteen

My hair's a mess, brushing it frantically in the bedroom mirror to make sure it falls the way Jayden prefers. If I don't look perfect, he'll go nuts, and I don't want anything to spoil my birthday night.

I've more or less moved in with him, now. He's even let me bring Samantha, which I know he didn't want to do. I think he got fed up of me talking about her so out of the blue one day told me to go get her, and I didn't wait for him to change his mind. I don't think I've ever run so fast in my life for anything. I know he's regretting it now, but it's too late, she's not going anywhere. The place stinks from her litter tray all the time, and the hairs on the furniture have to be cleaned daily, but I don't care. She's where she belongs.

Fly

The only thing that worries me, sometimes, is the way Jayden looks at her. It puts the creeps right up me. It's like he wants to kill her. His eyes turn really evil and his mouth grins, like he's thinking murderous, sinister thoughts. Samantha senses it I'm sure and does her best to keep away from him. I never leave her alone with him. I take her to work with me in a bag I've made. She hates it, but I don't take any notice of her. I'd never forgive myself if anything ever happened to her.

Sharon and all the girls at The Orchard love to see her. They were so sad when she left, so as I still bring her in with me, they've forgiven me - just.

Jayden, unfortunately, doesn't tire of letting me know how unhappy he is about his decision to let me bring her here. I should just leave her at The Orchard. I don't know why, but something, a sixth sense, tells me she'd be a lot safer there. I might ask Sharon.

Feeling fur on my leg, picking Samantha up and pulling her protectively to me, I would've been punched a thousand times over to have her close. If anything ever happened to her, I don't know what I'd do.

She hates it when Jayden's home. She snarls and hisses whenever he walks past her. He doesn't have to be doing anything, just his presence is enough. I think it's her cat way of trying to warn me about him, but I already know what he's like. I'm hoping I'm just being paranoid about him ever hurting her. I don't want to take the chance, though. My heart says he'd never hurt her, but my head is telling me something else.

Snuggling her close to me, feeling her soft fur on my lips, it tickles.

"He wouldn't hurt you, baby. Not on my birthday. He's only interested in hurting me. You're safe, I'm sure."

Purring as loud as a drum in my ear, I squeeze her tight. I love her so much it hurts; sure we're kindred spirits. Snuggling her to me, staring with revulsion at the clothes Jayden's laid out on the bed for me to wear tonight, Samantha meows in agreement, gently dropping her on top of the covers, watching her wobble to the middle of the bed and sit down. Picking each item up one by one, looking at them with dread, I'm having second thoughts about going out.

"What do you think, baby?"

Meowing up at me, licking her fur, I don't think she likes them either.

"Yuk, alright!"

Raising the blue, high-waisted, flared jeans to my waist, looking at them with horror, they are so old fashioned it hurts my eyes to imagine them on my body. Dropping them, and picking up an even older-looking, plain, mustard shirt that buttons right up to the neck, it has frilly short sleeves, gagging at how utterly revolting it is. Never in a million years would I have chosen anything mustard! I suppose the black pixie boots, next to my feet, are semi ok, but what good is that? No one's going to be that bothered what I'm wearing on my feet! The whole outfit is as far from sexy as you can get.

"Mustard frills! How fricking old does he think I am?"

The clothes he's choosing are getting worse, completely obvious he wants me to look unattractive, ugly, and *ancient!*

Reluctantly changing into them, inspecting myself in the mirror, I feel, and look, twenty years older than I should. Lola will laugh so much when she sees me later. I don't even want to guess what she'll say. Fluffing my hair, deciding a little bit of makeup might modernise what I've got on, the brown eyeliner I draw above and below my hazel eyes doesn't do much, deciding to finish the look off with a touch of mascara, but I still look old. Grabbing some lip gloss and dabbing some on my lips, it's a massive contrast to how Jayden prefers me to look in the bedroom. It's like he wants me to look like a saint when we're out, and a slut when we're in. He says it's because he doesn't want anyone else seeing how sexy I am.

He's made sure no one will think that tonight!

I'm not convinced that's the reason. He's jealous of everything, even my best friend. I can't say or do anything, ever, because there's always something he's not happy with. If I complain about these clothes he'll accuse me of not trusting what he chooses which will end in an argument. I'd rather look unsexy than be on the end of his fist.

Spraying myself with my favourite *LouLou* perfume, I remember some little sample pots Lola gave me the last time she went shopping, putting one of them in my back pocket just in case I need to spray myself later. I'm chuffed she was given so many of them.

Glancing around the bedroom, you wouldn't think I've moved in. Nothing much reflects me at all. Maybe the record player does, but Jayden likes music, too, so it could easily be his. There's not even a photograph of us together anywhere. It's his flat, so he's decorated it the way he wants, although I paid for nearly everything with my credit card, which he still hasn't paid a penny towards. I suppose it's a lot better than the bedsit he used to rent. The creepy guy in the Kermit the Frog vest had freaked me out so much, we'd had to move. That night is still so clear in my head. I've never seen the man since, thank God.

Rubbing my left cheek, reminded of the first time Jayden slapped me, it seems a lifetime ago, suddenly distracted by Samantha trying to navigate her way off the uncomfortable waterbed, which reminds me, I paid for that, too. I hated buying it. I didn't want to sleep, or have sex on anything that made me feel sea sick. I'd begged Jayden to change his mind, but he told me I'd get used to it, so I ended up buying the bloody awful thing because *he'd* always wanted one. Three and a half thousand dollars later, I'm still not used to it, and now I'm stuck paying the monthly repayments. He's always broke, or asking to borrow money. Tonight, he's asked to borrow another hundred dollars for I don't know what. I'm probably paying for my own birthday night out! He better start paying me back. My savings are seriously decreasing.

Opening my bedside drawer, grabbing the money, slipping it into my back pocket with the mini perfume sample, I hope this is the last time he asks.

Walking around the bed to my record player, my right foot hits something under the bed, bending, rubbing my big toe, seeing Jayden's brown box poking out from underneath. It's always locked, wondering what the hell could be inside. I've asked him a thousand times what's inside, but he tells me to, *'mind my own fucking business.'*

Slipping it away from sight, I walk to the far corner of our small bedroom where my record player and a handful of my favourite records, pre-approved by Jayden, sit in a neat pile next to it. *'Raw Like Sushi,'* by *Neneh Cherry*, has kept me company for most of the night, guessing I must've listened to it about a hundred times, now. I know nearly every word to every song, loving the lyrics, and *Neneh's* English accent. Who wouldn't. I don't think I've ever heard anyone speak with an English accent like hers before, except on the television. One day I'm going to England, especially London. It looks so cool.

Flipping on side one again, cleaning the needle with my finger, I carefully lower it onto the record waiting for the crackle, cranking up the volume before strolling to the kitchen to feed Samantha, who's already one step ahead of me, meowing all the way.

Dancing along to *'Buffalo Stance,'* preparing her food around the array of bongs and ashtrays full of roaches I still have yet to tidy up, the place stinks of weed, which I hate. Jayden smokes it regularly. All the walls and windows have streaky brown lines that stop half way down them that remind me too much of the walls in my house growing up. I don't know why he won't let me wash them; I've told him enough times how they make me feel. He says he prefers them that way, which is a complete lie. I think he just wants to piss me off. I wouldn't put it past him.

Burnt knives I assume have been used for burning hash, sit on top of the hob, and half cut plastic bottles in the corner tell me I'm right.

Jayden uses so many drugs.

Fly

Bongs of all different shapes and sizes sit on top of worktops thick with residue from drugs he and his friends have used. The knives, black on the ends, have bits of old hash on them, picking one up and smelling it, remembering the time he'd made me try it. It was disgusting, and made my head feel like it was floating off my shoulders. I'd panicked when he'd told me to suck into the end of the plastic bong. I couldn't breathe there was so much smoke, and the smell and taste were revolting. He'd laughed at my panic, and had been mad I was wasting it. I hadn't thought it funny at all. It'd felt so suffocating.

I've never done it again, but he still does it. In fact, his drug habit is getting worse.

Replacing the knife where I found it, I hope, in time, he stops doing the harder stuff and just sticks to weed.

Squeezing the food out of Samantha's food pouch, her insistent meowing tells me she must be starving, bending down, and giving it to her, watching as she greedily pounces on the jellied meat. The smell of that combined with the hash, is truly repulsive.

Pushing Jayden's different drug tools to one side; it's a miracle nothing's gone missing in the flat. He invites so many people over after his shifts at work, it's hard to keep up with who's who. Luckily, they've all been trustworthy and have only come around for drugs, and to watch porn. I'm not allowed to socialise when they visit. I have to stay in the bedroom and read the book Jayden's left out for me until they've left.

I can always hear what they're doing, though. The music that accompanies the videos gives me a clue which one they're watching. Jayden leaves sexy nightwear out for me to change into so I look similar to the women in the videos they're watching. I never look like them. No-one could.

They're just a fantasy. His fantasy, not mine.

"Make sure you have the outfit on before everyone has gone, and remember, wear the makeup how I like it."

I hear glasses clink, smell the weed, and listen when they comment on a particular woman on screen. I know straight away which video they're watching because I've taken a sneak peek at them when he's out.

If Jayden knew, I'd be dead.

I always feel like shit when I watch them, but I can't seem to stop myself. I don't want to feel aroused in any way, but my body betrays me, actually responds to women as they go down on men, fucking them in their sexy lingerie, telling them what they want them to do to them. Jayden has so many videos. It's the girls on girls he likes the most. When they lick each other, go down on each other and suck each other's juices, he goes crazy. He especially loves them talking dirty to each other. I feel physically sick knowing he watches them, gets off on watching them. Why aren't I enough? Admittedly, they're all beautiful, and curvy with monstrous boobs, so unlike mine so why the fuck does he even still want me?

It used to only be books he looked at, but the videos have taken over. The more hard-core the better for him.

The worse for me.

When I'm in my room trying to read whatever he's left out for me, which is usually the Bible, the smell of the weed floats under my door, and I start humming something in my head to make me feel better. I close my eyes and hum to whatever tune comes into my head. I managed to hum most of the songs from the Dare album the last time it happened. By the end song most of his friends had gone, and I was near enough asleep. He wasn't happy.

However much he's smoked and drunk determines the mood he's in, and I can guess that by whatever outfit he's left out for me to change into. He has favourite films.

He thinks the clothes are sexy. *I don't!*

I only wear them to make *him* happy, *not* me.

At first, I thought it was a bit of fun.

Now it's just boring.

I'd love to go to bed like everyone else, but Jayden's anything but normal. His appetite for sex is way too much for me to keep up with.

Fly

If I don't do what he wants, I know what will happen, and I guess it's easier to dress up in some stupid clothes than get a fat lip.

One time, I left the room to ask him a question. I was only in my pj's and had wanted to ask him about the outfit he left out, but he'd freaked, and dragged me back to the room by my hair. The men who were there just sat watching and looked away, not one of them tried to help me. I'm sure they must've all heard when Jayden threw me hard against the door. I'd never done it again.

Still clutching a bong I'm tidying away; the phone ringing makes me jump.

Three hours later, sliding Neneh back into her record cover, I leave Samantha lying on the bed and walk out to the small patio to water Jayden's rose bush which refuses to die. God knows why. He said it's the only thing he took from his old home after it burned down. His poor mother died in that fire. Perhaps he took it to remind him of her.

Far from wanting to go out now, it's late and all I feel like doing is taking off these awful clothes and putting on my pyjamas and snuggling up with Samantha. When Jayden phoned a few hours ago and told me not to eat anything, I thought he was on his way to take me out for my birthday dinner. Hearing him knocking now, I don't even want to let him in, but if I ignore the two double taps followed by three single taps, he'll bloody flip.

Running to the door, fake smiling, and letting him in, he looks me up and down, nodding as he heads towards the bedroom. Shining under the light, his hair is glossy and wet looking and not in the usual ponytail. It looks like he's just had a shower, yet he's been to the movies. He's left his hair long, letting it fall just above the collar of his favourite black leather, tassel-jacket, which has little droplets of water running down the back of it. Looking out the window, I don't see any rain. I always think he looks like a rock star in the jacket. That, paired with his tight black jeans that are now clinging to his thighs and groin, which I can't stop looking at, always reminds me of one of the men from *Mötley Crüe*, not that I like any of them. They are definitely *not* sexy. *Adam Ant* has always been my crush, now and forever. Not that Jayden knows. He'd kill me.

Seeing me eyeing up his groin, he smiles seductively at me.

"Like what you see, baby? You can eat me later."

Cheeks on fire, averting my eyes as he smirks and takes off his jacket, he practically flings it on top of Samantha, who jumps off the bed and lands at my feet. Sweat stains on his dark-grey, short-sleeved, silk shirt stink of stale perspiration, but I don't tell him.

His arms, full of Māori tribal tattoos, make him look tough, like a warrior. He's proud of his quarter Māori heritage and has told me his dad was half Māori and his mother was white. That must be why he's so good looking.

I was sad when he told me they'd both passed away, especially his poor mother who perished in the fire. I would've liked to have met them both. He's never really told me much about his mother. I wish he would. I'd love to hear about his years growing up. He's very secretive about it, which doesn't help me. It would be so much easier for me to understand him if I knew something. I've told him loads about my mother and what she was like.

Focusing on him and his shirt, two buttons undone at the top expose black, curly, chest hair perspiring with little droplets of water. His sweat mixed with his favourite Kouros aftershave is *yuk*. Unfortunately, the au de weed is stronger, adding to everything. Samantha must smell it, too, because she meows loudly and starts walking to another room. Kicking her in the leg as she passes, Jayden laughs as she lands on the hallway wall, her hissing and growling, showing her fangs and backing away from him. Wanting to kill him, his eyes warn me not to say anything, quickly walking to her and picking her up, pulling her to me, distracting him from her.

"Where did you get your long gold chain from? Is it new? I've never seen it before."

Shining bright under the light, it makes him look like a pimp, but

Fly

I don't tell him. I don't tell him about the smudges of mud on the tops of his black, shiny, pointy shoes either.

Ignoring my question, grunting, glaring at Samantha, he grabs his jacket and puts it back on.

"Got my money?"

The back of his jacket still has streaks of wet on it, following them down his back as he walks from the bedroom to the lounge. Turning, he extends his hand, me smiling nervously, flinching as I quickly give him the hundred dollars from my back pocket. I don't have the guts to ask why he always needs to borrow money. He's definitely not in the mood to say anything about it tonight.

His eyes like radars, scan the different rooms to see any evidence of what I've been doing, glaring at me; panicking, wondering whether I've left everything in the right place. Dividing the money into two piles as he walks from room to room he places half in each of his back jean-pockets, suddenly stopping outside the kitchen, turning, eyes pulsing straight at me.

"Who the fuck asked you to rearrange my bongs?"

Why the hell didn't I leave them alone?

Waiting for me to answer, he doesn't give me the chance, grabbing my arm, grunting at Samantha as she jumps to the floor. Dragging me to the front door, the top of my back feels the force of his push, stumbling, asking him to wait for me to get a jacket, but it's too late. He's already locked the door before I can say boo. I didn't say goodbye to Samantha, either, faintly hearing meowing from behind the door. My heart cries. I want to make sure she's ok.

Nearly falling down the two flights of stairs, his push is aggressive, finally making it out onto the street as he snatches my hand before the interrogation I've been expecting starts.

"So, what have you been doing since I rang? Watched any television? Read any books? Listened to music? *Spoken* to anyone else?"

What I really want to say is:

"*Oh, I've been helping myself to your hash, watching your stash of porn and frigging myself off.*"

What I do say is:

"Nothing much, just tidying up and getting ready. Samantha and I listened to a bit of *Neneh Cherry* on my record player."

Nodding, his eyes are more intense than usual, staring, scaring me as a strong gust of wind rescues me, sweeping me off balance, making him grab my wrist to steady me. Rubbing both arms with my hands, I want him to notice I'm cold, but all he does is reach into his jacket pocket, smile, and pull out a perfectly rolled joint for us to smoke on our way. Smiling back, I don't let him know that inside I feel the exact opposite.

How will it affect him tonight? I'm already worried, and I haven't even had a puff.

Smoking, especially drugs, is something I always thought I'd never do. I feel paranoid and anxious when I smoke and don't understand people who say it relaxes them. When I have it, I feel anything but.

Wind picking up, he cups his hand around the joint, trying to light it; I secretly pray to God that the wind continues, but my pleas are ignored, suddenly stopping for a miniscule of a second which gives him enough time to light and inhale deeply. Looking at the lit joint like an enemy, he waits for me to take it from his extended hand, laughing as I splutter and cough. My hair nearly catches fire having to quickly flick it to one side to take a second clumsy toke, coughing again, handing it back to him as passers-by give me disapproving looks.

I wish their judging eyes would die.

The smell, really strong, like sweet grass burning, probably means he's packed it full of female heads, which also means I'll be completely off my head very soon. Passing the joint back and forth, I feel extra light-headed already from lack of food, having to grab Jayden's arm for support, him flinging me off, sucking hard on the end of the joint until it's only a tiny lit roach, which he lodges in-between his first and second finger. Forming his left hand into a fist, he sucks as hard as he can through a miniscule hole he's made, the tiny roach

Fly

flickers against the wind as he sucks, amazed he is able to get anything out of the small thing poking from his fingers. Suddenly pointing his clenched fist at me to see if I want one last toke, I flinch, shaking my head from side to side, rubbing my hands up and down each of my arms again to make them warm. His eyes laughing at me, all he says is, "more for me, then," inhaling one last time, holding his breath and throwing the tiny roach to the gutter where the wind snatches it before it lands, whisking it away to who knows where.

I wish it was me it was whisking away.

Yanking my wrist hard, the click clack of my pixie boots walking fast, and the noises around me begin to amplify as people passing look at me intently. Staring into my eyes like they are looking right through to my soul, I don't want anyone, especially men, looking anywhere near me, or my bloody soul. I'm already anxious enough without having to worry about where Jayden's eyes are wandering.

He's always watching me.

Staying hyper focused, staring straight ahead, I do my best to avoid looking at anything or anyone. At this rate, I'm worried whether I'm even walking in a straight line.

Ten long minutes later, freezing, and stoned, Jayden stops and points to the club lights across the road. I've hardly listened to a word he's been saying, praying he'll give me his jacket, but he still hasn't noticed how cold I am. Following his pointed finger, the lasers coming from the top of the club are, I hate to admit, awesome, totally mesmerised by the red and green lines moving in time to the beat of the music coming from inside. The weed, taking full effect, has changed my mood and now I'm light and fuzzy and not cold anymore, feeling warmth travel down my entire body right to my groin. I don't want to go anywhere near the club now. What I want is to feel skin on skin, giving Jayden my best come to bed eyes, him staring at me, a lascivious grin not leaving me guessing what he'd like to be doing, too. Eyes boring straight into mine, his hands grab me around the waist, pulling me in close for a passionate kiss - right there - on the street, not caring who is watching. Gently taking my hand, smiling, he whispers, "Happy birthday, baby. Let's go," thinking he means home, for a teeny tiny second, I'm ecstatic. But he means the club, and my ecstasy turns to disappointment, not daring to show how sad I really feel. Pulling the tiny sample of perfume from my jean pocket, smiling, and spraying myself, I'm hoping it masks not only the smell of the weed, but my face, too.

"Mm Loulou. You can spray more of that when we get home."

Winking, taking my hand, he leads me across the road to the club.

Joni, the huge doorman I met when I first came to Wellington, is standing at his usual place letting people in. I would usually stop and say hi, but instead, I stare straight ahead, blurry eyed, conscious he might notice their redness. I'm sure he smells the weed masked with perfume from the way he keeps coughing, darting my eyes back and forth, just catching his eyes as they bore into mine. Moving his hand over his nose, I just see it from the corner of my eye, but don't look his way.

I'm not getting into trouble tonight for anyone.

Joni told me a long time ago that he's over to play rugby for the local team in Wellington. I think he earns extra cash here at the club to send back to his family in Fiji. Everyone who comes to the club loves him, except one person.

Jayden hates him, and Joni despises him back. Joni has told Lola that he can't see what a lovely girl like me is doing with someone like Jayden. He's told her how he wants to smash Jayden's ugly smug face in, and that he's seen him leave the club with different girls week after week at the end of his shifts, saying he knows he's up to no good.

Joni knows Lola will tell me, which she does, but that's not proof enough for me.

I need to see it with my own two eyes to believe it.

Joni would say anything to get me to break up with Jayden. He's not happy with how I'm treated, and has told Lola I deserve more respect and love. I know he loves me like a sister, and only wants what's best for me, but hating my boyfriend is only going to make me want to have less to do with him. Doesn't he know that?

Fly

I've always felt protectiveness from Joni, but the way he's treating Jayden is too much. He can't control who I go out with.

Recently, I've heard from Lola, that Joni's told her he's met a love of his own. Apparently, they've been going out for ages, although I've never seen her. I've never seen Joni with anyone, so, whoever it is, must be special. I'd like to meet her, but I don't think he wants to bring her here. It's most probably because of Jayden. He'd make Joni's life a living hell, and Joni wouldn't be able to control himself. It's practical to keep whoever it is a secret, which is a shame.

Standing in line, waiting to be let in, Joni's eagle eyes follow us until we are near. I know it kills him to see me like this; I'd much rather not come, but Jayden insists we come here instead of a different club. Deep down, I know Jayden enjoys seeing what it does to Joni. It's just another thing for me to have to worry about, watching the tension between the two.

I know I've changed a lot since meeting Jayden, and I'd love to stop and say hello, and joke around with Joni like I used to, but I can't. It's too much for me to cope with, and the interrogations afterwards from Jayden would only end in me getting a fat lip. It's best all round for me to just ignore Joni and keep myself safe. Lola's told me that Joni's told her that all I look these days is hollow, desperate, and high.

I hate that.

I've never told Jayden how Joni feels about him, but I don't really have to. It's obvious by the way they treat each other. One day, who knows, they might come to a truce. I miss sharing jokes and hanging out with Joni like I used to.

Nodding, releasing the rope and adding two clicks to his counter, Joni stares straight into Jayden's eyes.

He's not afraid of him.

Eyes locked like two silverback gorillas about to fight; I can't breathe watching them hold each other's gaze for approximately three seconds before some more people queue up to be let in.

Yanking my wrist hard, Jayden pulls me into him, making me

flinch, thinking I've done something to upset him. Staring at me without blinking, I panic listening to Joni yelling from behind.

"If only you knew, you bastard. If only you knew what I have on you. You wouldn't look so smug, believe me. You just wait, just wait! *O iko, au na vakamatei iko!*"

Jayden screams back.

"Yeah? I can't wait; you *prick*. Bring it on. *Mahi atu!* Go on then? Two can play your game."

Staring ahead as Jayden drags me towards the stairs; the dread I felt a few minutes before has magnified, daring to look back with questioning eyes towards Joni who is a raging bull ready to charge. Pushed up the stairs and through the door at the top, I can't stop thinking about what Joni just said.

What could he have on Jayden?

Ricki, the club owner, is there to welcome us just as Hithouse's electronic beat sends everyone mad. '*Jack to the Sound of the Underground,*' bangs out, and I don't want to picture anything but turning right around and leaving. Watching Ricki's old body moving in time to the music makes me want to laugh out loud as he twirls, giving everyone, including me, a poker chip for a free drink. Winking at me, placing another one in my hand, he tells me to go order a drink at the bar as he pats Jayden on the back and takes him to one side for a quick chat. I know better than to risk my life doing that so, instead, I wait, grabbing my chance to quickly look around.

DevO's is buzzing tonight, which I didn't expect. Thinking back to other Wednesday nights I and Lola have come here; they were dead in comparison. I'm guessing tonight must be a promotional night for some new drink, although I can't see any evidence of it.

A little club right in the heart of Wellington, I found DevO's when I first arrived and have been a regular for the past few years, even introducing it to Lola when she moved to the city. Practically every Wednesday since, her and I had jumped a cab to Manner's Street, and even popped into Candy's, a little bar right next door for a few drinks before we went upstairs. That was before I met Jayden.

Fly

I don't go anywhere near Candy's now, or out with Lola.

I miss those nights.

Popular with all ages, tonight DevO's looks full of students which Ricki seems particularly happy about.

Great for him, not so great for me.

The more people, the more focused I have to be not to look anyone's way. Very hard in a packed room when you're stoned. Finding a place to sit is going to be pretty slim.

Suddenly stiffening, Jayden's hand around my waist is tight, coming around and staring at me with questioning eyes. Stopping a passing member of the floor staff, he successfully arranges a little table for us very close to the bar which overlooks the dance floor, him pinching my waist to let me know he's watching everything. Looking straight ahead, following the back of the male staff members head to our table, Jayden pinches me again when I sit down at the three-seated table. Looking towards the dance floor for Lola, thinking she could use the extra seat, I instantly regret it.

"Having a good look around? See anything you like?"

Glaring at me, it's so hard for me not to look away. The fact I'm stoned isn't helping.

I lower my eyes to the floor.

"That's better. Keep them there."

I hate Jayden so much sometimes.

Approaching the bar to buy our usual, I swear I can feel his eyes burning through my skull like acid. Even though mine are on the floor, I know he's watching, waiting for me to screw up.

Focusing on my chewed, red-raw and sore nails, I gnaw at the skin around them, quickly hiding them under the table, hoping Jayden hasn't seen me. He likes my hands to be groomed and especially hates seeing them chewed. If he's seen me, he'll ask to inspect them, and then what will I do?

Playing with my fingers, I'm always on edge, constantly feeling I might do something to piss him off. The weed isn't helping, making me more paranoid than ever. I'm sure he laced it. He's done it before.

He loves tricking me into taking other drugs and once gave me pills for a cold. The night he tricked me into taking magic mushrooms was the worst. He cooked them like normal mushrooms and made me eat them, even though I wanted to be sick. It was horrible, horrific. Clenching my butt, amazed the muscles down there still work, the thought of that night still makes me tremble.

Paranoid that people can hear my thoughts, smell the weed, and see my eyes, all I want is Lola. Where is she? She said she'd meet me here.

Every muscle focusing on the table, I wait, ignoring the music and hum of people talking around me, relieved when seconds later Jayden returns with a double vodka and coke for me, and a double Jack Daniel's and coke for himself. Clinking glasses, looking into each other's eyes, his are smiling, but I know they are saying something very different.

I lower mine to the floor.

Jayden seems to know everyone, waving to different people, trying to see them from the corner of my eye. Smiling at men and women I don't know; I can only guess they are regulars he's met from working here at the club. It's his night off, too, so I suppose he's bound to know loads of people.

I often wonder why, of all the clubs in Wellington, did he have to walk into the only club I ever came to?

Girls wearing next to nothing approach the table giving me the once over before planting a kiss on either side of his cheek. Sitting at the extra seat we have, one of them lets her eyes linger a bit too long on Jayden's face; I want to react, but instead all I do is keep looking straight ahead pretending like nothing is happening.

The animal roaring inside me wants to pounce on her, rip her apart, glaring, daring my eyes to move. What she is wearing is so different to what I'm wearing. Jayden's eyes are all over her, taking in every bit of her monstrous cleavage. There's so much flesh on show, so much make-up. And don't get me started on the spiky, black, punk-looking hair and bright-red lipstick. She and her friends look more like hookers. If I dared dress like that, I wouldn't be allowed to walk out the door, yet he sits, ogling, openly flirting with them.

The cunt. I hate him. I hate them all.

As the hooker lookalikes leave, Jayden quickly grabs my wrist.

"Why isn't your head down?"

I can't help myself.

"Who were they?"

Thumping the table with his left fist, shaking, looking right at me, his eyes bulge out of their sockets, staring without blinking into mine, warning me I'll suffer if I ask any more questions. Shaking his head from side to side, his leery smile is anything but happy.

Staring back, defiant, even though I know I shouldn't, I watch his lips move through gritted teeth.

"No-one you would know. Why are you asking?"

Holding his stare, I've pushed it too far, backing down and looking to the floor. Suddenly his hand on my wrist drags me up from the table.

"Let's dance."

Trying to resist, it's no use. The last place I want to be is on the dance floor, begging to stay, telling him I feel sick, but he ignores me, squeezing my wrist even harder.

Stumbling, bumping into people as I'm pulled towards the dance floor, the double vodka and coke I skulled is making me feel even higher. Eyes fixed on the back of Jayden's head; my mood perks up a bit recognising the next song coming on. Greg the DJ is mixing one of my favourites. Not looking his way for fear, I fiercely want to give him the thumbs up as *Black Box* suddenly blasts out of the speakers above and the floor starts trembling to the beat of the familiar intro to '*Ride On Time.*' Hundreds of dancers explode in agreement and for a split second, I'm happy.

From nowhere Lola sashays onto the dancefloor with her usual entourage of men. Looking as beautiful as ever in a white satin suit, she looks like an executive. Why the hell she is wearing a suit? It's as far away from what she usually wears as she could get.

Looking a little closer, she's wearing nothing underneath her jacket; everyone, including me, gawp at her and her beautiful breasts jumping to the beat with abandon. Hair pulled up into a tight ponytail, her cheekbones show off her perfect oval face as she pouts, channelling her inner diva to everyone around her. Running up to her and hugging her, I'm so happy to see her, raising both thumbs in the air, closing my eyes and bouncing away to the beat as Greg spots our secret dance move and gives us a thumbs up, too.

I remember spending one whole night at his booth watching people dance with him. We'd decided that the thumbs up would be our secret code for letting him know whether I liked the song he was playing. Seeing his thumbs up in the air, I know he knows I like his choice, having told him enough times in the past how much I loved the song. He knows what's going on with Jayden, and I know he hates it. He's confessed how much he hates Jayden to Joni, who's told Lola, who's told me. Greg says he wishes Jayden was dead.

Just another one to add to the list.

Greg's also told Joni I've changed, and how much he misses me, and the laughs and jokes we used to have, especially the talk about music.

He must know I do, too.

He must know how much it kills me that I don't even look his way now.

The song ends, and *Boy George* suddenly blasts out into a solo before the beat of the song starts. I know Greg's playing it for me.

Suddenly, Lola's high-pitched voice in my ear distracts me.

"What the fuck do you have on, granny? I thought we were here for your birthday, not you auditioning for a place in an old people's home. Ha!"

Glaring at her, my eyes beg her to stop, feeling myself being pulled away from the floor as her head shakes and her hands ask what she's done. Jayden hates her and the attention she draws towards me, snarling at her as he drags me away.

Looking up to the DJ booth, Greg's head is shaking from side to side the same as Lola's. I recognise the look in his eyes, the one that tells me he's been in love with me forever, but I've never really loved him back, except in a brotherly way. I wish so much I could feel something more. I know deep down that he'd treat me right, but the spark has never been there, not the same as when I'd met Jayden. If I could zoom back to when I first met Jayden, I'd tell myself to run the fuck away and give Greg a chance.

It's too late now. I can't change it.

Back at the table, ordered to sit with my head down, Jayden goes to buy more drinks.

I don't want any more to drink.

I don't want anything.

I want to be home, with Samantha, not around people who might get me into trouble.

Most of my friends have tried to help, but they're all getting fed up, probably sick of their words falling on deaf ears.

I'm not deaf, though.

I can hear them.

They must know I'm too scared to listen.

Don't any of them know that?

The more they push me away, the more they push me towards Jayden. The only person I really have left now, is Lola but, pretty soon, I'm scared she'll leave, too.

Out of nowhere a man approaches my table, smiling at me.

What the fuck is he doing?

Praying he doesn't stop, I don't know why, but I look across to Greg for help, hoping Jayden hasn't seen me, snapping my head to the bar, thankful he's in conversation with someone. Suddenly the crowd explodes to the opening riffs of 'Ready to Go,' by *Republica*, looking to Greg, meeting his eyes; I know he's put it on for me again.

He knows how much I love Saffron.

By now most people, especially men, know what's going on. They know not to approach, or even look in my direction, but the one walking towards me obviously doesn't have a clue.

Does he want to die?

Well-dressed in casual jeans and a tight black t-shirt, he suddenly stops and asks if he can sit for a bit.

Why is he looking, talking to me? Go away, *please*. Please, just go before I get killed.

I shouldn't be looking anywhere near his face, but he's caught me off guard and the scars on both sides of his pale cheeks are too ugly to ignore. Thin frame, solid legs, and arms full of tattoos, his deep-set brown eyes, dark rings under each, look at me with nothing but kindness as he moves from side to side, like he needs the toilet. The stubble growing along his long chin where a few stray grey hairs peep through, doesn't match his pitch-black, almost shiny hair gelled back to an inch of its life. He has warm eyes. I know he means no harm.

Shaking, listening with dread to his deep voice, my heart wants to leave my body and run.

"My feet are hurting badly from all the dancing; do you mind if I sit for a minute at your table? You have three seats, and I see there are only two of you."

Jerking my head to the bar, seeing Jayden is in conversation with a woman, my head springs back to the man who's still looking at me. Lowering my eyes to the floor, his hand extends to me, introducing himself.

"I'm Mac. Nice to meet you."

Humming a song inside my head, closing my eyes, trying to ignore him, I start rocking back and forth, looking over to the bar again with dread.

It feels like my heart is ripping through my skin.

Seeing Jayden is still in conversation with the woman, he's holding the drinks which means he's getting ready to return to the table. Quickly making my way to him, I lightly tap his shoulder to let him know I need the bathroom while the woman's dagger eyes warn me off. She's the least of my worries, ignoring her, making my way to the loo before Mac gets me killed. I'm hoping Jayden will deal with him before I get back.

Fly

Watching from the back as Jayden approaches the table a few seconds later with the drinks; Mac turns as white as a ghost, standing, staring, looking into Jayden's eyes like he knows him. Does he? Was he planted here by Jayden to catch me out?

Mac's eyes switch from Jayden's face to his right arm, his own left hand rubbing his right shoulder, looking from himself to Jayden, shaking his head. Suddenly spotting me watching from the back, Mac eyes me.

Who the hell is he?

Apologising and backing away from Jayden, he makes his way into the middle of the dance floor, never taking his eyes off him. Hurrying back to my table, already worried for my safety without adding to it by taking too long in the loo, Jayden's already in conversation with another woman.

Frantically searching for Mac, Jayden sees me and immediately tells me to sit and look down to the floor.

Doing as I'm told, what the hell is going on?

Still watching from the corner of my eye, Mac bumps into Lola on the dance floor who's also witnessed the exchange. Staring into each other's eyes, for a moment, I think they're reading each other's thoughts.

Are they?

Nodding, Mac makes his way to the door, but just before he leaves, he takes one last look back at me and cuts across his throat with his thumb.

What the hell does he mean?

Two hours later, as *The Beatles* sing, '*Hey Jude*,' Jayden and I dance slowly, arms wrapped around each other, looking into each other's eyes with love. Pulling me in for a passionate kiss, it's the last song of the night, disappointed when the song ends. I love it when he's like this. It actually feels like the first time we met.

The last two hours have been nothing but wonderful.

Unusually calm, we hug long and hard, squinting at the harshness of the lights as they come on. My hand feels warm in his as he leads me to the exit, hardly hearing Greg as he wishes everyone a good night, very nearly missing Lola standing underneath his booth, waving, mouthing happy birthday to me as we pass. Smiling to her, I don't say anything, feeling a bit mean. It's not that I don't appreciate what she's said, I just don't want anything to spoil my night.

I can guess why she didn't approach me again all night. It was probably because she sensed it was best not to. I do miss having a laugh with her. Even though our nights were mostly spent watching men drool over her, we were still together. I hardly see her at all now.

Walking straight ahead to where Ricki waits to say goodbye, I smile and wave at him before clumsily walking down the stairs to where Joni is saying good night to people at the door. His sharp eyes watch our every move, snarling at Jayden like a lion warning off its prey as we pass. Luckily, this time, Jayden doesn't take the bait, not even looking Joni's way as he salutes and walks out of the club onto the street. I don't think he wants anything to spoil our night, either.

Happier than I've felt in a very long time, we whisper sweet nothings to each other, deciding to jump a cab instead of walking the fifteen minutes back to the flat.

The ride home is sensual, romantic.

This is the side of him I love, miss.

Five minutes later, walking the two flights of stairs up to the flat, we laugh and joke, even stopping on the stairs for a long kiss. Jolting for the toilet as soon as I'm inside, I shoo Samantha off who's come to say hello. My woozy head, and the bright light of the toilet is making my eyes squint, humming *'Hey Jude'* to myself as I pee, trying to decide what I will wear for our sexy night ahead.

Bang!

The toilet door slams open like a bomb has suddenly gone off, just missing my face.

Samantha growls.

Oh God.

Fly

Standing directly above me, staring down, Jayden's black eyes don't blink. Holding a huge packet of salt and vinegar chippies, his left hand slowly guides them, one by one, into his mouth, chewing slowly.

Oh God.

I should've known this would happen. I should've guessed. He promises it will never happen again and again, and I believe him time after time, giving him chance after chance. Tonight had been so perfect.

Why had I let my guard down?

I don't know what to do. I can't escape and know what's coming and can't stop it.

I can't get out.

Staring up at him, my brain thumping like it has a heart, he eats his chippies, his eyes pulsating, staring straight down at me, like a wolf eyeing up its next meal.

I pee myself.

Sliding down the wall, not taking his eyes off me, the door suddenly bangs hard against the wall, his foot pounding it again, making me jump as he's still eating, not blinking. His voice, eerily calm, is the complete opposite of his frantic hands and eyes.

"Why were you talking to the guy?"

I can't escape. *I can't escape.*

Fuck!

Deflating, my heart stops.

Flicking my eyes from side to side, searching for air, swallowing a hundred times to breathe, I don't know what to do.

"W-w-what guy?"

I can't breathe.

Jeans still around my ankles, Jayden blocks my exit.

The walls cave in.

I'm trapped.

Waiting, staring, crushing chippies between his fingers, I can't do anything.

Waiting, staring, waiting, waiting, staring, panic.

"The guy you were talking to at the table? The guy you wanted to *fuck* when my back was turned. *The guy whose number you probably have, now!*"

"W-w-w-what guy? I-I-I don't know who you mean."

Stomach in knots; my head feels like it's inflating with air, watching him watch my face, his eyes wide with anger. Every expression, every twitch makes him look possessed knowing those eyes from another monster in my past.

I'm done for.

"You - wanted - to - fuck - him!"

Peeing myself again, not taking my eyes off him, he waits for me to answer.

I can't take anymore.

I need to get out before he kills me.

"No! He only asked to sit at the table because his feet were sore. I didn't know what to say. It wasn't my table. I didn't talk to him. I didn't do anything."

It's too late for an explanation.

"So, you *do* know who I mean, you fucking bitch. Did you get a good look at his dick? *Did you like the look of it?*"

Crushing the chippie packet with his left fist, spraying me with its contents, he quickly stands up over me; raising both my arms, trying to defend myself, screaming.

"Slut."

Grabbing my head, he rams it down hard on his upturned knee; hearing the crack as my right eye comes into contact with it.

"Arghhh."

My legs like jelly, I try to stand and fight back whacking him as hard as I can with both hands, but it's no use.

"Leave me alone. Leave me alone, you fucking psycho."

It only makes him angrier, feeling the floor as he throws me down and grabs my hair with his right hand. Left hand in the air ready to punch me, his eyes suddenly change, like a child

Fly

watching a horror film, releasing my hair from his grasp, and running off.

Thud.

My head hits the floor.

Head spinning, splitting in two, there are little black dots everywhere as everything around me turns black. The last thing I hear is my mother's voice echoing off the walls.

"No-one will ever want you, you good for nothing little bitch."

Waking minutes later, the pain in my head, and around my right eye, is excruciating.

Am I dying?

Jeans still around my ankles, I slowly bend to pull them up, but the pain in my head is so bad, I have to steady myself on the wall and drag myself up. Something's inside my eyes making it impossible to see. Breathing, trying to ignore the pain, I blindly feel my way along the walls, reaching the bathroom, finding the light switch while my head splits in two. Sliding my jeans up, not bothering to fasten the button, I lift my face to the mirror not believing what I'm seeing.

Only one eye stares back.

What has he done to the other one. Where is it.

I can't think.

It's not me. *It's not me!*

I can't look like this.

I have to leave. I have to get out.

Staring, head throbbing like it's going to explode, my right eye is puffy and engorged with blood. It looks like I've done ten rounds in a boxing ring, touching it, wincing. The skin is squishy and the little slit that was my eye, is trickling with blood down my face.

What has he done.

Tracing my shaking fingers around my battered nose, my left eye is already starting to darken; my bottom lip is ripped and bulging ready to burst with blood, too.

Vomiting into the sink, my right eye wants to burst.

How the hell am I going to get away. I have to run. I have to run, get out of here. But where? He'll follow me. He'll follow me until he finds me, and then he'll kill me.

I don't know what to do.

What should I do?

Hearing crying from another room, slowly dragging myself to where it's coming from, Jayden's lying on the sitting room floor rolled up into a ball with both arms wrapped around his legs, rocking backwards and forwards, repeating over and over.

"It wasn't me. It was *him*. I didn't want to hurt you. *He* told me to watch while he hit you. I didn't want him to hurt you. You have to believe me. I couldn't do anything. *He* wouldn't let me."

Bending down, ignoring my head ripping in two, I wrap my arms around his shoulders and lay my battered head on top of them, soothing him like a baby while he cries.

"It's ok, you didn't know what you were doing. Shhh."

My head, brain, everything is in pain as my blood drips on his clothes. I have to make sure he is ok.

"I love you. Don't worry, shh, shh."

Turning, looking up at me, he's another person. Confusion etched on his face; he screams up at me with frightened, childish eyes, very different from fifteen minutes before.

"*Get out!* You're disgusting! I feel sick. Go away, leave me alone. *Get Out!*"

Rocking backwards and forwards again, screaming at me, I use his body for support to stand, dragging myself to the bedroom, stopping in front of what I think is a picture of Jesus, touching His face with my bloodied fingers before staggering into the bedroom. My face and hair full of blood, I prepare to die, collapsing on the bed as my mother's voice echoes all around me.

"*Not even God will want you. Happy Birthday, you ugly little bitch.*"

A gentle meow in my ear prepares me for death ...

Chapter Five

Abused people cling to their abusers.

— *Robert Galbraith*

Looking into the mirror, still patting concealer onto my right eye, I wonder what Mac is doing now and whether he knew what would happen to me that night? I'm sure he did. I'm sure he knew exactly what Jayden was capable of doing which is why he cut his throat with his thumb. It all makes such perfect sense now. The roaring of a motorbike panics me, standing up, looking out the window to see if he's home. I don't want to see him yet; thankful it's just some joyrider playing about. Falling onto the chair, shoulders hunched, breathing in and out fast, trembling.

I'm still amazed I didn't die that night. I really thought he'd done it. How ironic it would've been to have died on my birthday. God, Gail, a great grandmother, whoever, had other plans for me. Why I was allowed to vomit for three days into a bucket left beside my bed, is anyone's guess. My head had felt like it was splitting apart every time, guessing it was in as much shock as me.

Jayden had slapped, punched, pushed me into walls and stairs, you name it, but that night something changed. Jayden changed. He'd never hurt me on that scale before. Ever. A simple slap had turned into a near death beating, and it had only taken a matter of months to escalate. It happened so fast.

After that beating, I couldn't do anything for days. When I'd finally been able to lift my head to speak, Jayden had sat beside me on the bed, looking into my battered face, proudly showing off a sorry card he'd bought. I seriously think he'd expected me to be happy, grateful. He must have known I'd wanted to run, leave him before he killed me, but his childlike face had just sat, waiting for praise, watching me, even though he knew what he'd done was beyond disgusting. It was like nothing had happened.

I should've left him.

I should've known right then that things would only get worse.

That should've been the last time he'd ever laid a hand on me, but like so many times before, I gave him a second, third, fourth, fifth, sixth chance.

My right eye has never been the same, and the headaches that followed were, and still are, the worst I've ever experienced.

I admit, if I had died that night, I'm comforted by the fact that Jayden would've finished Samantha off, too.

Poor Sharon had been beside herself with worry. She'd left message after message on my answerphone begging me to call. When I'd finally been able to go back to work, two weeks later, she'd taken one look at my rainbow eye, and ordered me to come back to live at The Orchard. The girls had wanted to kill Jayden. Lola had even begged me to come live with her.

"*He'll kill you. He'll hit you one time too many and you'll die. You have to leave him. You have to. Please. Come live with me.*"

I wish I'd gone. I wish I'd run the fuck back to Sharon - to the girls - to safety - to love.

I don't know why I forgave him ... again.

I still don't know why.

Fly

I don't know why I'm here, getting ready for him ... again.

I don't know anything anymore.

Hearing Jayden's voice in my head, it bounces off the walls, quickly covering my ears with my hands to stop it.

Why is it always there?

"I love you so much, baby."

"I don't want other men to look at you the same way I look at you."

"I want you all to myself. Don't go out with Lola tonight. Stay with me. I want you here, with me."

"*Stop!* I don't want to hear it. *Stop!*"

Nearly breaking the legs of my chair, I rock back and forth hating myself for not having the guts to say anything to him. Why do I keep telling myself he's saying those things because he really wants to spend time with just me?

Why do I keep pretending he loves me?

"No one will ever want you. Not even God."

It's because of *her*. It's because of my *mother*. Her voice is constantly there, inside my brain, sure I'm still with Jayden because she's the last person I want to be right. If she could see where I've ended up she'd laugh and tell me that all the things that have gone missing in the flat are because of Jayden, and not to be stupid and believe everything he says. She'd tell me our two bikes, cd player, leather jacket, and camera, have been sold for drugs, and I know she'd be right, but as I don't have any solid proof, how can I confront him? I've even given Sharon Gail's necklace to look after just in case he sells it. There is no way I'm taking any chances of losing it, especially as I've seen him eyeing it up. If it goes missing and I accuse him of taking it, he'll punch me, even though my gut knows I'd be right. My gut knows he's probably sold everything, but I don't want to suffer another beating like that, ever again. I just accept everything without questioning anything because it's easier than getting a fat lip.

. . .

When I think back to the first time Jayden and I met, it's all so clear, now. Within days he was asking about money. How could I have not put two and two together? I didn't know he was fishing for information about my savings. How could I have known what he was doing? It wasn't like I'd had a boyfriend, anyone before him. I'm sure he knew that.

Everything he did was done so subtlety. He'd seemed genuinely interested in how much I earned at The Orchard, and even told me it was so he could compare how much we earned.

How was I so naïve?

I'd answered him like a school girl trying to impress her teacher; told him everything he wanted to know. I didn't once think it was being asked for anything other than wanting to get to know me. After that, he started asking to borrow a few dollars to keep him going till payday, and then a few dollars turned into a few hundred, which turned into a few thousand, until all my savings were completely wiped and I had to start stealing from The Orchard.

I'll never forgive myself for hurting Sharon the way I did.

I thought Jayden would pay back every penny. He hasn't, of course. Every week, like a fool, I handed over my wage packet which he opened in front of me and counted out a measly fifty dollars, handing it to me for buying toiletries etc. He'd said it was to 'teach' me to budget and to keep an eye on things that we needed to buy.

I hadn't even batted an eyelid.

I'd believed him.

I'd believed everything.

Of course, I had to show him receipts for everything I bought, and if things didn't tally up, I had to explain why. If he didn't believe me, then the walls and floor were all I felt.

I smoked drugs he brought home not once questioning how he'd paid for them. Of course, I knew, but said nothing.

I thought losing him would kill me. I couldn't lose him; he was all I had.

Fly

I gave into every need without blinking and changed who I was for him, turning into a person *he* wanted, not who I wanted to be.

Now, I just accept that money is always tight and don't dare ask where it's going or why there's never any left. I've even managed to get a credit card. Don't ask me how. Even when Jayden told me his time in jail wouldn't allow him to apply for one of his own, I didn't even question why he was in jail. Those words just bounced off me because all I cared about was pleasing him.

"No one will ever want you the same way I do. You're nothing without me. Nothing."

The more he tells me that, the more I believe him.

My mother pretty much told me the same thing my whole life, so there is absolutely no way I'm going to go back to being someone nobody loves.

I won't.

I can put up with all the beatings in the world.

It's the sex I hate more now than anything.

In the beginning, it was gentle and lovely. He was so giving. Jayden was so skilled in the bedroom. I loved that he took the time to explore every part of my body; even the parts I didn't know myself.

Now, when he touches me, all I feel is revulsion, and anxious. The anxiety dominates everything. I feel completely worthless, hating myself for letting him treat me the way he does. I don't challenge him when he wants sex every night, even when I bleed. If I'm not in the mood, he accuses me of seeing other men. How the hell I can be seeing other men when he knows I'm locked up like a prisoner most of the time; it's laughable, pathetic.

His accusive eyes question me, stare at me without blinking, waiting for me to slip up. When I look into them, he's another person. He's a demon waiting to pounce. I've learned to avert my eyes from anything he might deem unacceptable, which is just about everything.

Walking down the street with him, something so simple, has me panicking. If I look at photos of men in shop windows, I'm afraid he'll see. He always sees. I have to avoid looking in papers, magazines or on the television in case he sees my eyes move for a tiny second from him, or where they're supposed to be looking, which is straight ahead. I've convinced myself he has spies watching me, waiting for me to screw up. He's probably got people looking through the window at me, now.

Sometimes it's impossible not to look at pictures on the street, in shop windows, on the television, and I end up looking guiltier for doing nothing because I'm so anxious at what he's going to do. I learned very early on not to comment on anything on television or films, the interrogation afterwards so brutal. I thought he was joking, but he wasn't.

"Which one did you fancy? Did you get a good look at his dick? You want to fuck him, don't you? Don't you?"

Now, I make sure to look away. His eyes linger, waiting to catch me out. I'm always on edge. It's always about sex, twenty-four seven. It's got to the point where I feel I'm not even allowed control of my own thoughts.

Walking straight ahead, eyes dead, I'm like a living zombie.

I miss my friends and Sharon so much. I loved working at The Orchard. It was a place I felt safe, happy, and I had people who loved me. I finally felt I was in a place that I was accepted. I didn't think it would be a problem me working there, but Jayden soon put a stop to it. He was never happy that I had to talk to men every night, and now I know why. He got his way in the end.

Sharon and the girls were distraught, and kept ringing me every other day when I left.

They haven't given up, but don't ring nearly as much, now.

After seeing me with bruises more times than they could count, I think they've figured, if I don't care then neither do they.

I wish they would keep caring.

I'd do anything to still be there with them, now.

Fly

. . .

Phone calls I receive from anyone have to be put on loudspeaker so Jayden can hear everything, one call from Lola ending in me being thrown across the room in a rage so fierce, I ran out the door, down the stairs afraid he was going to kill me. I didn't even realise I'd wet myself until I'd stopped. All she'd done was tell me about a man she fancied.

The day that happened a friend of Jayden's had unexpectedly knocked on the door at the exact same time his hands were around my throat. Jayden's eyes were so terrifying, I swear I'd seen the devil.

Someone, maybe God, sent his friend at the exact time they knew I would die, but I wish God hadn't. I would've told God that keeping me alive was way worse.

When the doorbell rang, something in Jayden's head just flicked. He took his hands from around my throat and snapped out of whatever trance he was in, and then he casually answered the door and greeted his friend in a voice so normal, I'd thought I was going crazy. Maybe I was. Maybe I'd imagined he was trying to kill me. He was so different, nothing like the monster from five minutes before. One minute his hands were around my throat, and the next he was greeting his friend and leading him into the sitting room like nothing had happened. I listened to them joke, laugh, and talk, and his friend was none the wiser that I was in the next room frightened for my life, gasping for breath.

I ran that day, but I couldn't go anywhere, or to anyone, so I sat in the park, cowering, cold, confused, hungry, hating myself. It was dark when I finally returned, and like so many times before, I suffered the consequences.

Where could I go? Everyone, including myself, was sick of me.

Now it's night time I fear Jayden the most. His unnatural fantasies and addiction to pornography and drugs has grown. When he watches it, I feel even less human than I already do. It's like I'm a possession, a toy to be used and played with, and wonder if that's how he wants me to feel.

I'm not sure.

I'm not sure of anything these days.

I've been here before; when I was fifteen. I never thought for one minute that my boyfriend would turn out to be worse than the pervert from my past.

I've started cutting myself, again. It relieves the numbness, and if I'm honest, I like the feeling the pain gives me. I stopped it for a while, when I was at The Orchard, when I was happy. I've started to do it again because I'm anything but. I'm in hell. Even when I was living at home with my insane mother, it was better than this.

Jayden knows I cut myself, and gets angry if it interferes with his sex. If I suddenly start bleeding he goes ballistic, and I get more than a slap. He doesn't care why I cut. He doesn't care about anything but himself.

All he cares about, is sex, and his porn, the one thing I truly, truly hate.

I hate that he finds other women enticing and wish they'd just fuck off and leave me alone. I think he likes the fact that I get so jealous and deliberately watches the videos to make himself feel just that little bit more special.

It always ends up being about him.

Finding his stash of magazines is so easy. His imagination for finding places to conceal them isn't overly imaginative. I rummage through the wardrobe as soon as he leaves for work and find his brown box and piles of magazines, usually underneath a load of clothes in the corner. Penthouse, Mayfair, Men Only, Playboy, Fiesta, Knave, Jugs. It amazes me why women degrade themselves so much for men.

He reads them in bed at night when he gets home, and hands me a book of his choice, which is usually the Bible, to read right beside him where he can watch what I'm doing. Why he gives me the Bible

Fly

seems such a contradictory thing to do. Him reading his magazine, full of naked women, pretending to be interested in some article someone has written about cars, or whatever else he makes up, and then there's me, next to him reading about Sodom and Gomorrah. I try not to laugh. If only he knew I'd already read most of his stupid magazines.

Sitting in bed, taking in every curve, every ounce of flesh, he drools over the women's naked bodies and tells me in great detail what he'd like to be doing to each and every one of them. I've seen the women he is describing, the images stored safely in my head. I look straight ahead at my Bible pretending to read, and I see the blonde with the big boobs, the brunette with the big brown eyes and great ass, the redhead with silky smooth skin and nipples you can see through her top. Those images are projected onto every page I'm reading, and I wonder if God can see them and if so, then why isn't He doing anything to stop it. Why isn't He helping me.

I hate them. I hate them. I hate them.

I want to grab the magazines from Jayden's hands, rip them to shreds, burn them, throw them at his perverted face, scream at him, hurt him as much as he's hurting me. But all I do is nothing because I'm terrified of him. I lay there, my head near enough ready to explode, the lump in my stomach growing heavier by the minute. I don't dare show any emotion, but instead store all those feelings with the many before, the voice in my head screaming for him to stop reading. I can't risk even glancing at them. I know what he'd do. I'd only ever dared look his way once.

"*Whore! Who said you could look. Slap. Read what I've given you, or else.*"

I hate him so much, but I hate myself more.

Magazines aren't enough, so now he watches his videos, sometimes for hours. I have to lay with my head under the sheets until he's 'ready' for me.

Sometimes, it's so hot I can't breathe. Claustrophobic, suffocating like I'm in a coffin above ground, Jayden holds my sheet down with one hand while his other hand plays with himself above until he becomes so aroused, he turns me over and uses me like a piece of meat. He, of course, continues to watch the women on screen, and after he's finished, I'm thrown away like an old rag, but, he makes sure the covers are still over my head. I lay there, frozen, unable to move in fear, not even allowed to clean myself of his juices which dribble down my legs, cold and sticky.

I smell his lust, hear every orgasm, all the dialogue entrenched in my brain knowing the cue for when he will 'need' me again.

Today, I am a smutty nurse, one of his particular favourites. I'm allowed above the sheets, now, but I'm still not allowed to look anywhere near the screen. He has no idea I've watched the videos when he's out. I'm sure they're the reason his depravity reached depths not even I thought were possible. The night he raped me he ensured I was drugged with magic mushrooms he'd cooked first. I didn't know they were magic mushrooms when he'd forced them into my mouth. I was in the bath enjoying my soak, and he'd barged in and told me to eat them.

They were so disgusting, so grainy, like they'd been coated with sand. I let him think I'd swallowed them, but he made me open my mouth, and I'd spat them out into his hand and tried to kneel up to gag. That was stupid of me.

"Put them back in your mouth and fucking eat them."

"I don't like them, they taste weird, really grainy. What did you cook them in?"

"Put them back in your fucking mouth, or else."

I didn't have a clue why he was being so aggressive over a few mushrooms, but his raised hand had warned me to do as I was told, or else. So, I'd swallowed them while he held my mouth shut, checking my mouth was empty before he'd walked out of the bathroom.

An hour later, dressed in a red lace teddy, suspenders, and stockings that he'd left out, I remember touching up my makeup and finishing sticking my last long red fingernail onto my left thumb when the room suddenly, without warning, spun upside down. I'd

Fly

panicked, screamed for him to call an ambulance. He'd just walked into the bedroom and laughed, telling me I'd only had a few magic mushrooms and to enjoy the buzz.

I couldn't believe he'd tricked me.

"*What the fuck? You gave me drugs without telling me? What kind of fucking arsehole are you? You know I didn't want to try them. I told you!*"

"Don't worry, baby, I'll look after you. Just enjoy it."

That's the last thing I remember.

The next morning, I'd staggered to the toilet; my body aching all over. The last thing I remember was the room spinning upside down and him telling me about the mushrooms.

Sitting down to pee, the throbbing pain coming from my backside was so intense I'd stopped breathing for a second. When I'd wiped myself it had felt like I was being ripped apart by shards of glass from the inside.

I felt sick.

I tried to clench my butt, but the pain was too much; I had no control of that region. There was blood all over the toilet paper, thinking I was dying. I'd always told him that was one thing I never wanted to do. Ever.

I couldn't walk properly for days afterwards, the pain was so bad, I couldn't even sit, and had to lay on my side whenever I could. The girls at work kept asking what was wrong, but I was way too embarrassed to tell them the truth, so I just told them I had piles. Jayden thought it was the funniest thing he'd heard. He told me I'd wanted him to do it, that I'd begged him.

Had I?

I knew that was something I would never have agreed to.

He wanted to do it again, without drugs so I could see how good it felt. He pestered me for days, made me feel guilty until I gave in. I knew I didn't really have a choice so, because I was still sore, I told him I needed something to numb the pain and stupidly agreed to smoking a strong joint to feel a little more relaxed.

It remains the single most horrifying moment of my life to date.

Screaming in agony, howling for him to stop, the glass shards ripped me apart from inside, again. Jayden only agreed to stop because there was so much blood, even for him. I think he was worried my screaming would make the neighbours call the police, so he'd muffled my cries with his hand and spoken ever so softly in my ear while his other hand had finished himself off.

He threw me aside like a piece of trash, wiped his hand on my back and walked off.

"*You look like shit. Go and clean yourself up, and change the fucking sheets.*"

Chapter Six

Sometimes we refuse to see how bad something is until it completely destroys us.

— Unknown

Looking out the window, humming anything that comes into my head, I clench my butt muscles without even thinking, thanking God they still work. Jayden's never gone anywhere near that region again, and I haven't touched any kind of mushrooms since.

Another motorbike zooms past, thinking it's him. I'm sure the one I hear now in the distance is his. I'd recognise the sound of the engine anywhere.

Don't ask me how. I just do.

Sitting back down in front of the mirror, I'm not sure my head, heart, or skin, can take anymore. I'm pushed and pulled in so many directions these days; I don't even know if where I am is real. I'm going mad with all the accusations, jealousy and control. I haven't done any of what he says, sure he knows how terrified I am of him, but I always end up looking and feeling like I'm guilty, which makes it worse. It's the fear. It betrays me, makes it seem like I'm lying when I'm not.

These days I just accept my lot and get on with it. Who cares, anyway? No one's really interested, and if I'm honest, I wouldn't either if I was them.

I'm even sick of myself.

In my head I know what Jayden is doing is wrong, but I can't seem to unglue myself from him. It's like everything has been sucked out of me and all I can think of is how to survive. I don't know how it's got this bad. I desperately want to leave him, but I don't know how. I don't know what to do. I'm terrified ninety-nine percent of the time, and I figure, if no one else wants me, it's the better of the two evils. At least someone, even if it is a psycho, wants me around.

Thank God I still have Samantha, my heart, the reason I'm still alive.

Finding my vodka and gulping it back in one, blood runs down my arm and lands on my dress again, watching it through the mirror. I hate my life. I hate Jayden, and I hate to admit, I miss Lola, who I haven't seen for what seems like a lifetime. I'd do anything to see her again. She was a bitch, but I knew she loved me in her warped way.

Anything is better than what I have now.

My miracle, my special someone I thought was just around the corner, has turned out to be the devil reincarnated. He's driven everyone I love away. If Gail was still here, it'd be a very different story. She was the one person who really knew me, understood why I am like I am, because her mother, my grandmother, was a carbon copy of my mother.

I still can't believe she was my aunt. Finding out she and my bitch mother had been long lost sisters, had rocked my world to the core and sent me down a spiral not even I could've predicted. Losing Gail had been so painful. I found, and lost my aunt in a matter of a day, unprepared for how much it would hurt.

Perhaps that's the reason I let Jayden destroy me. So, I don't have to feel the pain of losing her again.

Fly

Battered, bleeding, bruised.

Gail definitely would've told me to get rid of Jayden the moment she'd met him, and I probably would've. After I lost her so suddenly, I stopped listening to everyone. God knows Sharon had tried and tried to steer me away from him; so had all the girls, but I hadn't listened. I hadn't even listened to myself.

Everyone, including myself, hates him.

Jumping up, looking out the window, he's parking his bike, watching him dismount from his Ducati through the window. Taking off his helmet and smiling at people passing, anyone would think he was a normal guy. Little do they know what an evil fucker he is. That his heart is so black, even the devil would have trouble finding it. I don't know why I don't have the guts to run, like I did from my mother and the pervert all those years ago. I can't seem to detach from him, confused at what keeps me loyal. The last six months have been the worst of my life, even worse than living with my mother and the pervert combined. Jayden has mentally, verbally, and physically destroyed me with his control, his morbid jealousy, and possessiveness. Sometimes I wish he would kill me.

At least I'd be free.

Covering my fresh wound with my hand, the blood won't stop running down my arm, looking around for a plaster to stick over it.

"Fuck. Where are they?"

Walking the few steps to the kitchen, the red stilettos I have on nearly make me fall, steadying myself on the door frame, staining it with my bloodied hand, granny-stepping to the drawers to find some plasters. Slapping two on, quickly grabbing a filthy tea towel to clean the blood off my hand, arm, door frame and dress, the nails make everything I do so much harder.

Spotting another bottle of vodka on the work surface, unscrewing it, gulping as much as I can, my ankles scream, not used to the height. I feel awkward, uncomfortable. The only way I cope these days is by drinking. Funnily, I've never been able to stomach whisky.

Feeling like I've swallowed the sun, the vodka travels all the way through my body right to my fingertips. I'm woozy, just the way I like, but now I need to pee.

Republica's, 'Out of the Darkness,' is still playing in the background, humming along, stumbling to the toilet, using the walls as my support.

Ping. One of my red nails lands on the floor.

"Fuck."

Meow.

Samantha follows me.

Bang.

The front door slams shut, hearing his keys jingling in his hand.

"Precious. I'm home. Where are you?"

Precious? I'll never be his fucking precious. If I ever get out of here alive, I'll make sure I'm no one's precious, ever again, except Samantha. She'll always have my heart.

Meowing up at me, I want to pick her up, but instead shoo her off to the bathroom, clumsily closing the door, quickly scuttling towards the kitchen, and the vodka bottle, sculling back as much as I can before he finds me.

Awaiting the inspection, frozen on the spot, still needing to pee, the adrenaline is pumping, hearing the *crunch, crunch, crunch* of his boots which must have some gravel underneath them from outside. The noise is deafening over the music.

"*Shit.*"

Seeing my reflection through the metal of the fridge, I've forgotten to put my nurse's cap on. He'll kill me.

Rooted to the spot, pissed at myself for not putting the stupid bloody thing on, I hope he doesn't notice. Please, don't let him notice.

Jumping as he yells; I cross my fingers behind my back and pray.

"*That fucking music!*"

Striding to the stereo, turning the volume down, I wish he'd turn his voice to mute.

"Haven't I told you not to play your music so loud?"

Fly

Waiting, standing to attention in the cold kitchen, looking straight ahead, I see him eyeing my plaster and die inside.

"Where's the cap?"

Walking towards me, eyes fixed on my plaster, I'm praying he's in a good mood. My heart, thumping in my chest, wants to escape as he examines my face, commenting on my full, red, glossy lips, thick black eyeliner, and blue eye-shadow. The overdone rouge, he says, looks like a clown, but he'll let me off.

Brushing my cheek with his thumb, I flinch at his touch, his eyes laughing as he suddenly grabs me around the waist, causing my tight, white, PVC nurse's outfit to squeak. Roughly turning me around, he inspects my stockings for any runs, turning me back around and telling me the cap won't matter this time. Breathing out, uncrossing my fingers, I thank God, or whoever else, for small mercies.

Petrified Jayden's mood will change, I try to placate him.

"D-d-do I look alright?"

His fiery, glazy eyes home in on my breasts, drawn to a tiny speck of blood I've not cleaned off my cleavage.

I want to die.

Staring without blinking at me, his wild eyes pulse; his hands below rub my nipples hard, trembling at his touch. Without warning he bends down; his rough tongue tickling my skin as it laps up the speck of blood off my chest.

"Mm, sweet as."

Raising his hand, making me flinch, he thinks it's funny, raising his hand again for fun.

"Please, don't hurt me."

"Shut the fuck up. You're such easy work, no challenge at all. Just like my mother. You're *pathetic*."

Nearly falling, his rough hand on my wrist hurts as my feet try to keep up with him. The stilettos I'm wearing are making it impossible, begging him to stop.

"I need to pee, let me pee first, please?"

Landing on the bed with a thud, quickly kneeling up while he grabs the TV remote, the noises outside are quickly drowned out by the familiar sound of the hard-core porn he loves. It's times like these I hate him the most, grimacing as he yells at me to strip. This is the last thing I want to be doing. I still need to pee, begging him again to let me go.

"I'll be quick, I promise."

The prick isn't having any of it.

"Fucking strip."

Glaring at him, trying to keep my balance on the waterbed, I mentally will my bladder to hold as I unzip my pinafore and expose my tiny breasts, throwing it to the floor just as a woman on screen gasps and he looks away. Only in my G-string, stockings, and stilettos, his eyes approve.

I hate him.

Cringing inside, I don't want him, or his hands anywhere near me, panicking when he hardens at a buxom, blonde bimbo onscreen undressing another blonde busty nurse in the exact same clothes he's made me wear. Seeing them through the mirror, they are gorgeous, and curvy, him delighting in telling me so.

"Look at them. That's what I like to see. A bit of flesh. So much better than you, *you skeleton*. As you've gone to so much effort for me, I can't let it go to waste now, can I precious. Stand up, turn around, and bend over. You look better from behind. I like a woman with a bit more meat on her bones, a few curves. You were so much better when I first met you. *Stand up!*"

Doesn't he know his words are what keeps the weight off?

Nearly losing my balance scuffling to the edge of the bed, I'm petrified I'll pierce the plastic with one of my stilettos, wobbling as I come off, nearly peeing in the process. Pleading with him to just let me go to the toilet before I wet myself, he's not having any of it.

"Bend over."

Moving towards me, kneeling, inhaling my scent; his breath is warm, suddenly grabbing my G-string, ripping it off with force.

Fly

Licking me slowly, his tongue is soft on my skin finding what it seeks, him telling me I taste better than I look.

"Like a peach."

Repelled, my body still responds to him, giving in to what he wants, even making myself believe I'm enjoying it by imagining it's *Adam Ant* behind me and not him. Gasping as his hands suddenly grab hold of my hips and turn me around, he pushes me to the hard floor to kneel opposite him; his huge hands around my head hurting as they pull me towards his glistening mouth. Ordering me to lick my juices from his chin, I want to be sick, pretending to like the taste as one of the nurses on screen thankfully breaks his concentration by orgasming, him using my shoulders to stand up and watch.

My shoulders and knees scream.

Slowly unzipping his leather trousers, fully focused on the nurses onscreen, I know what's coming, quickly cleaning my mouth with my hand before looking up at his face, hearing one of the nurses as she orgasms.

"Please, just let me pee."

Grabbing my head; plunging it into his groin, he forces his hardness into my mouth; I want to bite, rip it off with my teeth, make him bleed. But I don't, letting his hands clutch my head and pull it back and forth in a steady rhythm.

I want to be sick.

He tastes dirty, just like the filth he's watching, and I can tell he's close to climax because his hands start pulling on my head, faster.

Meow, meow, meow.

Samantha! How did she get out?

Staring up, meowing loudly, I try to shoo her away as Jayden growls and throws me to the floor.

"That fucking cat."

"Don't hurt her."

Scrambling up from the floor, I fall on my stilettos; him laughing, bending down and grabbing Samantha by the tail.

Smash. Yelping in pain, she hits the wall and falls to the floor.

M.A. McNally

Thud.
Warmth trickles down my legs.
"Samantha!"

Vowing there and then to get revenge for everything Jayden has ever done to us, I can't know what is about to unfold. I can't know that the biggest can of worms is about to be opened, and the revenge I crave, want so much, will go on to cause so much personal inner conflict, that the decision I finally make, will change my life forever.

Chapter Seven

There is no safe way to remain in a relationship with a person who has no conscience. The only solution is to escape.

— Unknown

"Samantha! No! What have you done, you *monster!* Please don't be dead, baby? Samantha? *Samantha!*"

Meowing up at me, I gently pick her up, holding her close to my heart as her breathing becomes laboured. Gasping at the blood oozing out of her mouth and nose, I gently clean it away with my hand as her gentle meows turn to a whisper, staring into my eyes. I know she is saying goodbye. I can't breathe, holding her close, kissing her head over and over. She can't be gone. *She can't be gone.*

A second later, my darling Samantha meows for the last time; my world collapses as she goes limp in my arms and slips away.

"*No! My baby. My baby!* This can't be happening. It can't be happening. Please, God, don't let it be happening."

Rocking her in my arms, hysterical, my cheeks are wet with my tears.

"Samantha, stay with me, baby. Stay with me. I'll get you to a vet, soon. Don't be gone. Please don't be gone. *NO!*"

Closing my eyes, rocking her gently, she is a kitten, inside my top meowing up at me while I hoover my room. She's welcoming me home from school every day, meowing and rubbing my leg. She's lying on my bed, above my neck, rubbing my face, purring, and then she's soaking wet, like a drowned rat as I raise her up in the rain, telling her off. She's pouncing on food outside the train station, running away from me in the park, on Gail's lap, rubbing Sharon's leg as she bends to pat her; I can't stop crying. Samantha is my world, the only reason I'm still here. Please don't let her be gone.

Why. Why did I bring her here? Why didn't I leave her at The Orchard? I can't breathe. I can't do anything but hold her to me.

Laughing behind me, Jayden sneers.

"She was a waste of space. We're better off without her stinking out the flat. Bloody stupid cat. I'm glad to see the back end of the flea-ridden pest."

His words bounce off me, not allowing them to penetrate. They can't because I'm already shattered into a million little pieces.

I can't breathe.

Flinging my stilettos to the wall, picking myself and Samantha up carefully from the floor, I take her to the bed and rest her on top, snarling at Jayden as I change out of my wet stockings into any clothing I can find. Sitting back on the bed, bringing Samantha to me, cuddling her, the hole in my stomach is getting bigger and bigger by the second, and all I want to do is jump into it with her and stay there forever.

Watching me, Jayden wants to react, but something is stopping him. Is it guilt. I'd love that. I'd love for him to feel. I'd love for him to feel something other than lust or control.

I wish he'd die.

I wish I would die.

If I die, then the pain I'm feeling will go, and I will be with not only Samantha, but Gail, too.

Fly

I can't die, though. Not yet. He has to pay for what he's done.

He has to pay for what he's done.

Looking up towards him, he's staring at me with a look on his face that's confused, like a child who knows it's done wrong but isn't being punished. Coming towards me, I glare at him, grunting, daring him to come closer, and for once, he listens, looking away quickly, muttering under his breath.

"Fuck this. That thing better be out of here when I get back. Crying over a fucking cat. You're fucked in the head."

It's time for me to fight back.

"*Fuck off!* Leave us alone ... you *monster!* You're the one who's fucked in the head. *Not me.* What did she ever do to you? She was just a cat. Why? Why couldn't you leave her alone. Fuck off! Fuck off, and leave us alone. *Leave - us - a—*"

Before I know it, Jayden's hand is around my throat, and my head has banged so hard against the wall, I've nearly passed out. I've pushed it.

Holding Samantha tight, staring into Jayden's pulsating eyes, I don't want to do anything that might make him take her off me, backing down and looking away.

"That's right, bitch. You look away, where you're supposed to. You're lucky I don't take that stupid flea-ridden thing off you right now. You got just a little bit too far above yourself, didn't you. You better remember who's boss here, eh? Not you. *Me.* I'll let you off just this once because your pretty little pussy died, but don't ever speak to me like that again. *You hear?* You're lucky I don't throw it in the bin outside where it belongs. I used to like cats. Especially their eyes. Now, fucking clean yourself and that piece of shit up, before I do something I really regret."

Striding to the television, the porn he loves is still playing, switching it off before he angrily strides into the front room to collect his keys. Slamming the front door hard, forgetting to lock it, I lay Samantha on the bed and run to the window, watching as he jumps on his bike and zooms off.

I don't have much time. I have to get out before he realises what he's done.

Moving fast, quickly grabbing any clothes I can find and putting them in a bag, I run to the kitchen and find a box, coating the bottom of it with Samantha's brocade coat, laying her on it. Face saturated, hardly able to see through my never-ending tears, I frantically rummage through the wardrobe to find my favourite bobbly jumper of Gail's to put over Samantha, banging my foot on something hard at the bottom. Screaming, dragging out whatever I've hit, I look down at Jayden's old brown, battered box, grabbing it and stashing it in my bag. Whatever's in there will have to wait. If Jayden comes back now and catches me, I'm dead. Seeing his stash of magazines, I throw them all over the floor, grabbing some and ripping them up, covering the clothes from the wardrobe with them. He'll hate that. He'll hate his filth being treated like the trash it is.

Hearing a motorbike approaching, I don't wait, grabbing the bobbly jumper, Samantha and my bag, making a run for the front door, not even closing it. Racing down the stairs barefoot, clutching Samantha to my chest, the box is heavy, running out the entrance onto the street like my life depends on it. My bolt for freedom suddenly snatched away, two hands grab me roughly from behind.

"*No!*"

Chapter Eight

You left and forgot to tell my heart how to go on without you.

— Unknown

"Where the fuck are you off to in such a hurry, freak?"

Staring up into Lola's face; bursting into tears, blurting out words that don't sound like anything, she tries her best to calm me down. Following my hand pointing at the box, she looks inside, eyes wide, her quick intake of breath is all I hear as she pulls me in, hugging me close to her.

"Has he done this? Has he? I'll fucking kill him."

Nodding, all I can do is cry, trying to speak through my tears.

"T-t-take me to yours, please? Quickly! Before Jayden realises he hasn't locked the door. *Quick!* He'll kill me."

"Before he realises he hasn't locked the door? What the fuck, Jesse? I tell you what. If I see him, I'll fucking kill the cunt."

I've never been so happy to see her.

Hailing the first cab she sees, following her, and jumping in, I hide my head in case Jayden returns and sees me. Ten long minutes later, arriving at Lola's flat, we run up the stairs like our feet are on hot coals, breathing out when we are safely inside. Running to the window and shutting the blinds, Lola turns to me and tries to talk, but I'm crying like a baby, telling her again what has happened, choking on words I don't want to believe are true.

"My Samantha. She's gone. *She's gone.*"

Lola's teeth over her bottom lip, and eyes, which stare straight ahead, communicate she doesn't know what to say. That, or she's trying to hold it together for me. Maybe she doesn't know how to feel. She never really liked Samantha and probably doesn't care she's gone. She'd never tell me. She wouldn't be that cruel.

"We need a stiff drink," she says, guiding me into a seat by the window before running to the kitchen to fetch some glasses. The dust on the blinds is thick, separating them ever so slightly with my finger, staring out at the crowds below. My mind must be playing tricks with me because every person I see looks like Jayden, shaking when Lola hands me a glass, the ice rattling against the sides as I bring it to my mouth, still crying over the box at my feet. I don't want to believe Samantha is in it, that she is gone. Not my baby. How will I ever live without her?

Lola's voice suddenly interrupts my thoughts.

"We can't stay here. The prick knows where I live. He'll know you're here. Let me phone Sharon and see if she knows anyone or anywhere we can go until we can contact the police."

"No. I don't want the police involved. I just want Jayden gone. I just want to forget he exists."

"You know that won't happen. He'll find a way of getting to you, you know that, Jesse."

Listening as she phones Sharon; I know she's right. He'll find a way, and then what will happen. I need to make sure he doesn't do this to anyone else.

The noise of a motorbike has me on my feet, the glass in my hand nearly falling. I can't take it. I'm free, but for how long. How long will it take for me to change my mind and go back to him. I always do.

Fly

With no time to think, Lola takes the glass from my hand and gently guides my arm telling me we are going to a place Sharon has organised. Even if I want to go back to Jayden, I can't.

This is the last chance I'll get to make things right. If I ruin it, no one will ever help me again. I have to do this for them, but most of all, I have to do this for myself, and my Samantha.

It's time to fight back.

Chapter Nine

No one saves us but ourselves. No one can and no one may. We ourselves must walk the path.

— *Buddha*

Standing in the hallway of the most extravagant house I've ever been in, Roy, a good friend of Sharon's, welcomes us.

Crying in the cab the whole way, I hadn't really listened to Lola when she'd told me where we were going. I couldn't have imagined this, a massive house with huge chandeliers and draped, blood-red, velvet curtains, on the hills of the very affluent Karaka Bay.

It's like I've jumped into an old-fashioned book, the musty smell only adding to everything.

Walking Lola and I up the grandest staircase, Roy's gesticulating hands and high voice assure us we are safe and that no harm will come to us. Clutching for dear life onto the box still in my arms, crying all the way to my room, I panic when Roy tries to take the box from my arms, telling me in his softest voice that Samantha will have the best sending off money can buy.

Fly

I can't let him take her.
I can't let him take my baby.
I can't never see her again.

Screaming, thrashing my arms and legs with every ounce of energy I have left, Lola tries to calm me, but it's no use, I'm not giving Samantha up for anything.

Out of nowhere, two big, burly brutes grab me; Sharon suddenly appears with a needle, stabbing me in the arm, fighting her off, kicking and screaming, until I can't fight anymore.

―――――

A week later, lying in a bed I have no recollection of getting into, I slowly open my eyes, seeing Sharon and Lola sitting beside me, not knowing if I'm dreaming or if it's real.

In and out of consciousness for the next couple of days, when I finally wake I'm eventually told my body went into shock, and that I was days away from dying due to my organs shutting down from malnutrition.

Weak, wasted, worn out.

―――――

Weeks pass, gaining strength; every time I wake, I look for Samantha at the end of my bed, swearing I can hear her soft meow, smell her sweet oily scent. But she's not there. All that is there is the most beautiful black and silver urn which sits right next to my bed. The coloured urn, similar to Samantha's fur, sits on the table, and inside a round photo frame, in the centre, is a picture of her which has me in tears too many times to count.

She really *is* gone.

Somehow finding the strength to let her go, it is the second hardest thing of my life to do.

Sharon, and Roy, who I'm told is the boyfriend of Tiffany, a friend of Lola's, tell me in their sweetest voices that Samantha received the grandest, and most beautiful send-off money could buy. I'm grateful, but I wish they would've waited for me. I wish I could've said goodbye to my baby properly.

Determined to make things right for not only myself, but for Samantha, too, somehow, I find a way through all the sorrow, stronger and more determined.

Like a Phoenix rising from the ashes, the woman who stands before me in the mirror two months later, is ready to fight back. Kissing the necklace around my neck that Gail gave me, I'm so thankful Sharon kept it safe. Stronger, I'm hell-bent on making things right.

"This is for you, Gail, and Samantha. This is for us all. No-one will ever hurt me again. *Ever!* I'll make sure that fucker pays for everything he's ever done, especially to you, Samantha. Jayden will pay for everything!"

Chapter Ten

This was the vengeance for which she had longed, for which she had plotted, the vengeance she had at last achieved.

— *Shakespeare*

A few days later Sharon visits and tells me Jayden has been stalking The Orchard for the last two weeks, but not to worry, because she's right on top of it and has hired two of the biggest bouncers around. Undecided whether I'm hallucinating, the woman sitting in front of me sounds like Sharon, but her baggy, purple, track pants, pink glitzy hoodie, clumpy pink and silver sneakers, and short blonde wig, don't look like her. Shaking my head to see if I'm actually awake, I point to her head, confused, relieved when she quickly takes the blonde wig off and laughs at her mistake.

"Oh, I'm sorry, Jesse. Ha, ha. I borrowed the wig from one of the girls."

I want to laugh, but don't just in case she becomes angry, asking her instead why she's in disguise.

"It's to stop any of Jayden's friends from following me. He definitely won't look for me dressed like this. I make sure he does not know where you are. I promised Gail to keep you safe, and I'm not taking any chances."

She looks so funny, thankful to hear she and the girls are safe. But I know hiring bouncers and dressing up in different clothes won't stop Jayden from finding me. None of us are safe until we know where he is and what he's doing. He has so many criminal friends you never know what he's going to pull next. Sensing my apprehension, Sharon tries to reassure me, patting my hand with her wrinkly fingers.

"There is no way Jayden is getting anywhere near you, or The Orchard, so don't worry. I think he's finally got the message you're not there, because I haven't seen him for the last couple of days. I was smart and asked my police friends to come a few times."

Tapping her nose, I know who Sharon's talking about. Her police friends are the same officers I saw talking to the girl whose job I replaced at The Orchard the first day I walked in there. If it weren't for her walking out that day, Sharon would never have given me the job. It seems a lifetime ago that I was terrified of those cops. I thought they were going to take me back to my mother. How could I have guessed that two years down the line, they'd be instrumental in protecting me from another psycho. Like dealing with my mother wasn't enough for one lifetime. Sharon, of course, tells me she has given the cops a few freebies for helping her out, but I know that won't stop Jayden from finding me. He'll find me if it's the last thing he does. There is no way he is going to give up without a fight.

Plucking up the guts days later to venture outside for some fresh air, Sharon's worried someone will see me.

"You wear wig and different clothes so no one will know it's you, Jesse. Lola will walk with you, too."

I have to admit I'm petrified; looking behind me every five seconds to see if Jayden is there. How do I know he hasn't bribed people to find me? These days I'm constantly torn between missing him and hating him, which I know Lola isn't finding easy.

Eyes pointing north more often than not, she hasn't told me what she is obviously thinking, but she doesn't have to. Her gritted teeth and pained expression tell me all I need to know. I haven't challenged her, mainly because I haven't got the energy, and the fact she's practically been glued to my hip since she found me, tells me enough. She and Sharon don't want anything bad to happen to me; I love them for that.

Sharon hasn't batted an eyelid that Lola isn't working. She knows, apart from herself, that Lola is the closest person to me, and Sharon does have a business to run at the end of the day. She has to make sure the other girls are safe, too, even if it means sacrificing one of her best girls for a bit.

Ramona, I hear, has taken over the phone duties and is getting on better with Lola, who tells me they've even shared the odd day out together. Am I still hallucinating?

The other girls, I hear, are happy, too. With both of Sharon's highest earners out of action, it's given them a much needed boost in earnings.

Sitting on the end of my bed watching Lola's every expression, I'm not sure but I think there's something she's not telling me.

"Don't get *too* excited. When you were sacked and Ramona asked to take over phone duties, I started getting on better with her. I suppose not having her as competition helped a bit. She told me she didn't really enjoy being upstairs. Sharon was a bit peeved to begin with, but soon realised that having a beautiful girl on reception actually helped bring in business. We're busier now than we've ever been."

"Gee, thanks. Are you telling me I wasn't beautiful enough, eh?"

"Oh, shut up. You know what I mean. Anyway, I started chatting to Ramona a bit more and even managed to find out a little about her life growing up. You know, she had it tougher than people think. When she found out what happened to you, and especially Samantha, she was the only one who even asked how I was. Nobody else even cared. I think Ramona actually cared, and she was asking about you all the time. Still does. She's even given me the odd massage here and there, which has helped a heap. She's great with her hands. It's the least I could do being nice to her, aye. It doesn't mean I like her. I still think she's an up-herself bitch."

Listening to Lola trying to convince herself she doesn't feel anything for Ramona, is like watching an alcoholic say they don't like to drink. It's so obvious she's lying and likes her more than a friend, but I'm not sure why she's trying to hide it. If I'm honest, I don't really have the strength to challenge it. I'm more interested in finding a way to make Jayden pay for what he's done to my Samantha.

It feels like my heart has done nothing but cry since she's been gone. I still can't believe I'm never going to hear her gentle meow in my ear, or feel her beautiful soft fur on my skin anymore. The pain is even more excruciating than when I lost Gail.

Jayden knew exactly what he was doing when he killed her. He knew to have her gone would rip my heart right out of my chest. I hate him more than anything or anyone in this world. Even more than my mother and the pervert. How the hell am I going to make him pay for what he's done? I don't have the first clue what to do or where to look. He's a big bloke, with lots of big bloke druggie friends. It's not like I have any dirt on him that everybody else doesn't already know.

The lightbulb in my head pings, and suddenly I'm more than excited.

"*The box!*"

Springing off the bed like I've just stood on a live wire, poor Lola doesn't know what to do.

"Where's the box? Where's the box that was in my bag? Who's taken it? Who's taken it, Lola?"

Backing away from me, trembling, her right hand rests on her heart, tapping her chest as she catches her breath.

"What the hell? Calm down. Bloody hell, Jesse, you scared me

Fly

half to death. I thought you were having a fit. Thank God I don't have to do CPR on you. That would've grossed me out, *big time*. Your stupid box is safe, don't worry. Sharon locked it away in Roy's safe the day I brought you here. For some reason she didn't want anyone getting their hands on it. Like anyone would've wanted to go anywhere near it! It's old and looks dodgy, and don't get me started on how much it *stinks*. She told me the code to the safe in case you wanted it. Do you want me to go get it for you?"

Is she really asking me this question? Lips pursed, my head moves side to side, my slits for eyes and clenched fists give her the answer she's waiting for, but she's staring at me like she still doesn't understand. I'm losing patience.

"What do you think, Einstein? *Go get it. Hurry up!*"

Waiting, my heart is literally jumping out of my chest needing to know what's inside. Remembering it was locked, I race downstairs to find a hammer; poor Roy doesn't know how to react, grabbing it from his hand when he finds it, quickly running back up the stairs with him following close behind. Back in my room Lola is waiting next to the bed with the box in her hand, looking at it.

"Put it on the floor. Quick!"

Placing it in the middle of the room, Lola quickly backs away, wiping her hands on her clothes like she's caught a disease. Killing me with her eyes, I don't have time to care what she thinks, running, hammer raised above my head, whacking the lock hard once, twice, three times until it is broken off. Kneeling before the broken box, I don't know why, but I rub the necklace around my neck for luck before looking up at Lola's anxious eyes, nodding for her to come. Eyes fixed on each other, we each take a corner of the box and slowly open it together.

"What the hell?"

Roy gasps, Lola looks at me, pointing into the box.

"What the hell is that?"

Chapter Eleven

Pandora's box had been opened and monsters had come out.

— Lisa Marie Rice

"What is it, Jesse? It looks like a shrivelled-up eye. Is that Jayden in these photos? Who's he with? This cap stinks of weed."

Picking up the cap like it's contaminated, Lola raises it up using the hammer, scrunching up her nose as she looks at it from every angle. I pick up what looks like a dried-up eye with my free hand, inspecting it while Lola guffaws at the 'I love potatoes' emblazoned across the front of the cap. She's in fits of laughter.

"Who puts a heart on a hat saying they love potatoes? *Potatoes*. It's such a weird thing for Jayden to own, and don't get me started on the shrivelled up looking eye in your hand. It actually looks real."

Undecided whether it's a marble or something more sordid, I throw it back in the box near enough breaking the old wood as it rolls like a pinball off different things and settles next to the cap. Seeing photographs, I pick them up looking through seven, eight old pictures

Fly

of Jayden with a young girl who I think must be Maxine, the sister he rarely talked about. A letter addressed to her is still sealed, picking it up and turning it over and over, confused, speaking to myself out loud.

"Why would a letter to his sister be unopened? Surely he would've read it."

Still holding it in my hand, a bundle of rolled up cash sits next to what looks like a yellow fang, undecided if it's an animal's. This is getting weirder by the second. Moving it to the side with the hammer, rummaging right to the bottom, I find more photos and some folded-up newspaper articles of an abandoned baby which Lola snatches from my hand and starts to read.

"What the fuck? What the hell is this, and why does Jayden have clippings of an abandoned baby? This is getting really fucking weird."

Grabbing one of the articles from her, reading it, my eyes point straight at her without blinking.

"Have you seen the date the baby was born? Look. July the eighteenth. That's *your* birthday."

Snatching the paper from my hand and reading the article, Lola turns green, like she's going to be sick. Her eyes, fixed on my face, don't blink; it looks like she's holding her breath. Is she sick, scared? I'm not sure. Whatever she's read, it's spooked her out, pointing to the paper as she speaks.

"The woman who gave birth was found in a train station toilet. No way! No fucking way! It's too much of a coincidence. Jesse, i-i-is this article ... about me?"

Throwing it to me, backing away, shaking, I read on while she listens.

"Abandoned after a week, the mother, a young girl of sixteen named Abigail, slipped out of the hospital never to be seen again. All she left was a necklace."

Then I read what they named the baby and understand why Lola is staring at me.

"They called the baby, Zoe. This article is *about you*. OMG. *What the hell?* Why the hell has Jayden got this? It can't have been his. He was too young. It must've been his mother's. But why would she have cut these out. Why would she have kept articles about you. Why?"

"Get it away from me, Jesse. I'm too freaked out at the moment. I can't breathe. I can't breathe."

Running to a drawer to find a paper bag, I rush back to her, making her breathe in and out of it, gently patting her back until she is calm and able to talk. This is definitely not what I expected to find inside the box.

"Lola. The box your mum gave you that you keep putting off opening. We have to go back to yours to get it. We have to get that box."

Waiting for her to stop coughing, I can tell this is freaking her out too much by the way she shoves my hand away.

"We can't. What if Jayden's watching. What if he's sitting there waiting for us. It's too risky, Jesse. He knows you've stolen this box. He knows what's in it and you better believe he's out there trying to find it. You better believe he wants to *kill* you."

She's right. We can't go back, but, we can ask someone to go for us, and I know just the person.

Turning to Roy, he's shaking his head from side to side, pointing a finger at me, shaking that, too. Pleading with him to help, he's worried there might be people waiting to jump him.

"I'm not going anywhere near the place by myself. What if your psycho boyfriend is there. Or someone he's paid to kill you. How am I going to find a little box? I can't go. Tiffany will kill me. She'll definitely tell me not to go. No way. Never. Don't ask me again because it's definitely *not* happening."

Driving to the flat that afternoon with two, big, burly, bodyguards in tow, Roy finds the front door smashed open and the whole place trashed, ringing to let us know when he gets there. Telling us that every picture has been slashed with something sharp, Lola's more concerned about her stash of drugs, asking Roy to check her bedside drawer.

"It looks like a tornado has come in and scattered everything everywhere, Lola. I'm sorry hunny, but your drugs are well and truly gone. The only things I can see apart from clothes, are an empty wooden box with carvings and mother of pearl on it, and about ten smaller boxes that have necklaces and earrings sprawled everywhere. The empty boxes look to have had whatever was inside them, taken."

Screaming behind me, pissed about her drugs and jewellery being taken, I tell her to shut up, listening as Roy continues through the flat.

"Whatever you're looking for must have been taken."

Snatching the phone from me, Lola screams down the receiver.

"The box wasn't in my bedroom drawer. I got bloody sick of looking at it every time I opened it, so I buried it inside the arms of one of my cuddly toys. The fluffy elephant, right on top of the bookshelf in the front room? See if it's still there."

Sure enough, the elephant doesn't look to have been touched, and still sitting on top of the bookshelf, unharmed, safely tucked inside its arms sits a small white box. Opening it up, one of the bodyguards confirms there is something inside.

After Roy calls a locksmith to change the lock on the front door, he and the bodyguards make their way back to the house where they find Lola and I in the kitchen pacing back and forth anxiously awaiting the return of the box. Handing the new key, and a small white box to Lola, Roy and his bodyguards wait, as do I, for her to open it. Staring at the box in her outstretched hand, it is shaking like jelly.

"I don't know if I can do this, Jesse."

Grabbing it from her hand, I'm in no mood for her drama.

"Bull crap, you can't. Come on. Let's see what's inside once and for all."

Chapter Twelve

Pandora's box could not be unopened, no one could return to Eden.

— *Selena Kitt*

"It can't be. *It can't be.* This is a joke, Lola. It's got to be a joke, doesn't it?"

Our eyes, fixed on the necklace now dangling from my shaking fingers, stare in disbelief at an exact replica of the necklace Gail gave me the night before she died. Feeling the cold smooth silver of my own necklace around my neck, I touch the bump in the middle without even thinking, rubbing it before guiding the centre of Lola's necklace to my left eye. Seeing the Lord's prayer clear as day; I can't stop shivering.

"What does this mean, Lola? Why do we have the same necklace?"

Shaking her head sideways at me, her look is as puzzled as mine.

"I-I-I don't know, Jesse. I don't know."

Squeezing each other tight, arms entwined, we stare, stunned, silent, watching the necklace swinging in my hand reflecting the

Fly

brightness of the late afternoon sun. This has to be a dream that I'll wake up from soon.

"Take yours off, Jesse. See if they really are the same. Let's be sure they're *exactly* the same."

Taking mine off and laying both of them side by side on the kitchen table, we both stand, shaking our heads, turning to each other, not blinking as the reality of the situation sinks in.

"There's a reason for all of this, Jesse. The box, the articles, the unopened letter? There has to be a clue in it. There has to be."

Gazing at Maxine's unopened letter inside the box, I'm not sure if I can open it. The stress of losing Samantha is still hanging around my shoulders like a heavy cloak; I don't know if I've got the strength for any more heartache. But, seeing Lola's face and questioning eyes, I can see how much she needs me to do this. It's not about me today. It's about her and the answers she's so desperately wanted ever since she found out she was adopted. If opening this letter will bring her a few steps closer to some answers, then it will be worth the heartache. Grabbing the letter from the box, heart beating ten to the dozen, I hope I'm doing the right thing.

"Ok, here goes."

Chapter Thirteen
Patricia

A mistake made with good in your heart is still a mistake, but it is one for which you must forgive yourself.

— Linda Sue Park

Saturday July 1st, 1993

My darling Maxine. You've been gone four months, five days, six hours, and seven minutes; I miss you every second of every minute, of every hour, of every day. It's your birthday in just under three weeks. How am I ever going to survive?

I know why you ran. I will never forgive myself for being the reason. You were only trying to protect me from your brother, but both you and I know that you would never have had the strength to take on his monster. No one could, not even your father. The guilt eats me alive daily, and even

Fly

though I accept the beatings from your father and brother, it still doesn't compare to the pain I feel in my heart for causing you to flee.

I wish one of them would finish me off. At least I'd be with you.

My tears are never ending. They won't stop until I know you are safe.

Please be safe.

It's the middle of the night, and by some miracle, both your father and brother are fast asleep. I only have a small window before one of them wakes and comes looking for me. I've sneaked out to write this goodbye letter to you because I know if I don't, you'll never get to hear the truth. I need you to know the truth before your brother kills me. One day he'll do it, of that I'm sure.

I don't know why I haven't run, like you. I could leave, now, while they're both still asleep, but where would I go? No-one wants me, and I'm too weak to do anything. They've made sure of that. I deserve to suffer and often think I deserve to die for bringing you here. I was so selfish, only thinking of myself. I knew how violent and hostile your father was, yet I brought you here of my own accord because I wanted another child. I wanted a daughter. Forgive me darling, please?

By the time you read this, I'll be dead. I don't know why, but I feel it in my gut that I won't make it to see you again. Trust your gut, darling, it's never wrong.

I wanted to tell you so many times growing up how you came to be mine.

You see, I didn't have any intention of taking you, but

she begged me, your mother. She was so young, only sixteen at the time, and being on the streets, she didn't see what other choice she had. She asked me to take you to safety.

If only she knew.

I couldn't run the risk of taking you and your mother to my home. I wanted to, but your father would've killed me and you were already too precious to me.

I chose you, and left your poor mother on the toilet floor, in the train station for everyone else to deal with. It all happened so fast. One minute I was cutting your cord with a pair of scissors, giving you to her, the next you were wrapped up in a jumper, inside my bag, and I was carefully walking you out the door to the train.

I jumped on and dared not look back.

Of course, your father wasn't happy when I turned up out of the blue with a new baby in tow. I'd left him, you see, and had no intention of ever going back, but circumstances I couldn't have predicted changed that, none of which you need to know about. It didn't take him long to accept you, and I don't know why, but there was something about you that moved him, stopped him from hurting you. He responded to you differently than your brother. I'm still not sure why. Maybe he saw a little bit of you in him. You weren't his by blood, but for some reason you had the same spirit as him. You even had the same eyes, something I couldn't explain.

Jayden fell in love with you the moment he saw you. You made your brother change for a short time. Without you, I don't know what would've happened to him, to us.

I kept all the articles of the other baby, the one they

Fly

were trying to find the mother to. It was too much of a coincidence for it not to be your sister, your twin. When I left your mother on the toilet floor, she was close to having the second baby and said she didn't want both of them taken. She begged me to take you and wouldn't take no for an answer, so I gave in. I vowed no-one would know anything until my death, that you would be kept secret.

My darling, I think your sister is called Zoe. Find her. Find your sister and reunite with her. I know your birth mother would've wanted that. Forgive me. I thought I was doing the best thing for you when I took you home. I should've known your father wouldn't change. I should've known your brother would eventually return to being the monster he was, but I was too wrapped up in having the daughter I always wanted and knew I would never have. Your body still hasn't been found, so all I can do is hope that you've run as far away as possible. Please, don't ever come back.

I'm going to hide this letter in my secret box right at the back of my wardrobe where no one but me knows where it is. At least I have one thing that no one knows about. I'm sure your brother will find it when I'm gone. He has ways of finding everything. I just hope he gives you this letter. I hope you get to read it before him.

I'm so sorry you had to find out this way.

Forgive me. Please, forgive me.

You will always be my daughter. I will love you forever my darling Maxine Gail Rose, named after your grandfather, your birth mother, and my mother. I never told you that. I know I haven't been the mother you wanted, but please accept, you were always the daughter I dreamed of and wanted so very much.

I love you to the moon and back, now, and forever.

Your loving mother, Patricia Xxxx (The Angel Lady)

PS. The lock of hair in the box belongs to your birth mother, Abigail, although she liked to be called Gail. She wanted you to have it so you could smell it and remember her. She loved you so very much. I pray to God she is still alive and you find her.

Chapter Fourteen
Jesse

That was how dishonesty and betrayal started, not in big lies but in small secrets.

— *Amy Tan*

"It can't be true. *It can't be.* Gail can't be your *mum*. That would mean ... that would mean ... you're my cousin? That we're related. Lola, Maxine was Jayden's sister, which means he's *your* half step-brother? Surely not. He wasn't Gail's son, so he can't be any relation, can he? I'm so confused. I want to kill him for what he did to Samantha. I want that mother fucker to suffer. How can that happen, now? The Angel Lady. Gail told me the Angel Lady took her baby. Remember? You even asked me yourself who she was. This has to be true. I'm the only one who knew the Angel Lady existed."

Dropping the letter, crying, hugging Lola as tight as I can, we can't speak. We can't do anything but stare and touch each other's face, hair, eyes. Never in a million years did we think opening the box would tell us this. *Ever!* What do we do now? This will change everything. *Everything*. Pulling away, taking my hands, Lola's eyes are puffy from crying, looking at me with concern.

"This is crazy. It's a dream that we're both going to wake from, soon. I feel sick. Fuck me, thank God Jayden's *not* your blood cousin, Jesse. That would be *disgusting*. Truly disgusting. This sort of thing only happens in books, or films. Why of all the people in the fucking world did *he* have to be involved. *Why*. We're going to have to tell him. You know that, don't you?"

"Shut up! I don't want to think about it. If he was my real cousin, imagine if I'd got pregnant! I can't think about it because if I do, I'm going to be sick. It can't be real. This has to be some sort of joke. It's *his* sordid joke. Jayden can't be related. *He can't be*. I'll still fucking kill him for what he did to Samantha, to me. Sharon will know what to do. We have to tell her. What is she going to do when she finds out your Gail's daughter? That Maxine, Jayden's sister is Gail's other daughter, and *your* twin. She's going to freak!"

Staring into space, two lonely tears trickle in unison down Lola's cheeks, finding her mouth, where her tongue absentmindedly licks them away. The sadness in her eyes is enough to make me cry. I know exactly what she's thinking because I'm thinking it, too. Taking her hand, squeezing it tight, I smile, gently saying words that I still can't believe are true.

"You found your mum, Lola. You know who she was now. I can tell you so much about her, it'll be like you always knew her. Don't worry, I'll make sure you know everything. I've always felt there was something between us. I always knew."

Sucking her teeth between her lips, she doesn't know what to do except smile and take my hand, squeezing it tight. Breathing in, stopping her sucking, she gently says, "Let's go tell Sharon together. We'll show her the box. This is all so much to take in. Fuck me, I know who my mother was, and I have a sister who may or may not be alive. Sharon is going to freak."

I'm not sure I heard her properly, frowning, raising my eyebrows at her.

Fly

"We can't go there, Lola. *He* might be there. Jayden will definitely still be looking for me, and that's the second place he would've gone. You know that. Let's ring Sharon instead and ask her to meet us in the park around the corner from The Orchard tomorrow morning, early. We'll say it's mega important. Roy can back us up, can't you?"

Looking to Roy, he, and the bodyguards are all staring, open mouthed, nodding. Looking from me to Lola, Roy is shaking his head, jumping when Lola suddenly yells.

"*No!* I need to get out of here, get some fresh air. My parents will probably be freaking out because I haven't rung them for days. I'll need to clear my head before I can do that. I can't believe I have a *twin. A sister.* Family. I have to find her. You have to help me find her. You have to help me find Maxine."

Chapter Fifteen
Maxine

The scars you can't see are the hardest to heal.

— *Astrid Alauda*

I'm gaining strength. My saviour says I'll be strong enough to go out very soon. But I'm terrified. What if I see the pig who tried to murder me. I can't run the risk of that happening. I have to make sure he won't recognise me, try to kill me again. The scars are still visible. Thank God, they are fading. What the pig has left in my memory, though, is much deeper. I'll never forget. *Never.*

His face, his hand on the knife, the panic, the terror as the blade punctured my skin over and over. I won't feel safe again until the pig's been slaughtered.

My Saviour's been helping me, asking people he knows who work in prisons, police stations, bars, nightclubs, if they might know him. It's no use. Nobody knows anything. Surely, someone has to know. The scars, the melted skin.

Visiting the library as a last resort, my Saviour finds something. A lead, an article about a fire that nearly killed a family in Porirua

Fly

dating back twenty years or more. A young boy, Jonathan, barely made it out alive after being badly burned. The fireman thought him dead until he'd started whimpering. '*A True Miracle,*' they called it.

It's too much of a coincidence for it not to be him. The pig mentioned my brother when he attacked me. How did he know him? Was Jayden to blame for what happened to him? This all happened before I was born.

I have to find Jayden now, even if I don't want to. My mother. I don't know if she's alive. I have to go back, see if she's still there. Next week. Next week I'll ask my Saviour to take me.

Next week I'll find some answers.

Chapter Sixteen
Jesse

Secrets are made to be found out with time.

— Charles Sanford

Driving past The Orchard, making sure no one is watching, one of Roy's bodyguards pulls into the park around the corner. Dressed in men's clothes, and wearing short dark wigs, Lola and I quickly jump out and wait on the bench we've told Sharon to meet us at. Assuring us they'll watch from the car, both the bodyguards scour the place in case Jayden, or anyone else he might've paid to follow us, turns up.

I have to admit, I'm terrified, counting the minutes, waiting for Sharon, whose tiny body slinks around the corner a second later, like a cat following a rat.

Like *that* doesn't look suspicious.

Prodding Lola in the ribs, laughing out loud as Sharon's beady eyes spot us, Lola can't hold it in, laughing as loud as a foghorn as Sharon nods and walks slowly towards the bench. Prodding Lola in the ribs again, telling her to shut up, Sharon gently sits on the end of the bench, fiddling with her hair while she talks into the air and lights a long cigarette between her bony fingers, puffing the end of it.

"You girls safe? No one follow you?"

Pretending to talk between ourselves, we talk in low voices, loud enough for her to hear.

"Isn't the park lovely in the morning. *No one* around at all. I don't think there's a soul *except* us. I don't even think the birds are up yet."

Glancing over in Sharon's direction, smoke leaves her lips, which start to move, talking to nothing but the air.

"Ok, why do you want me here so early? This better be good. And why are you talking and dressing like men?"

Breathing in, nodding to each other, Lola and I start explaining what has happened the night before, watching Sharon's eyes become wider and wider. Unable to blink, staring straight at us, she throws her cigarette to the ground and does something so unlike her, we swear she might be an imposter.

Sliding up to Lola, taking her face in her bony hands, Sharon gently strokes it like a baby while tears roll down her wrinkly cheeks, leaving streaks in her make-up.

"Gail's baby? It can't be. It can't be. You are so beautiful, just like your mummy. You two girls I can't believe are related. This is a miracle. A miracle. Both of you are family, now. You are both part of my family."

Hugging, crying, unable to hold our feelings in, the last twenty-four hours have been like a dream, pinching ourselves to make sure it's real.

Suddenly Sharon wipes her face and looks at me like she means business.

"Ok, we need to find your boyfriend, ask him why he have the box. He needs to know Lola is his sister's twin. I know this is very hard for you, Jesse, especially because he hurt you, and your beautiful Samantha, but he is a big part of the puzzle, now. We must be careful, though. Until he knows, he will want to hurt you. He will want to hurt all of us."

As much as I hate to admit it, I know she's right. He'll be out there looking for us as we speak. I don't want to have to talk to him, but for Lola's, and now Maxine's sake, I have to find a way of getting him to listen without killing any of us. Somewhere public, and I know just the place.

Driving us to DevO's six hours early, Roy's bodyguards do a sweep of the street before giving us the ok to exit the car. Telling us they'll wait outside in case Jayden or anyone else turns up, we try to slink in unnoticed, but the doors are locked, knocking hard on the glass to see if anyone is there.

Running out, Joni's worried face unlocks the door, asking if everything is alright.

"What's wrong? Why are you here so early? I was just picking something up, so you're lucky you caught me."

Not prepared for what we tell him, the shock on his face is evident, especially when we tell him Lola and Maxine, Jayden's sister, are twins.

"Jayden's sister? Are you sure? You, Lola – Maxine's biological sister. His sister, Maxine? This has to be a joke, aye."

Looking like he's going to vomit; I tell him to sit down while Lola finds something to fan him with. It's the last thing I expect he thought he'd hear. He hates Jayden more than anyone in the world, so hearing he has a sister is probably a shock. Patting him on the back to see if he's up to hearing the rest, he nods to let me know he's ok.

"It's not a joke, Joni. It's real, and now we have to find the bastard and tell him before he kills us. Don't get me wrong. Jayden still has to pay for what he did to me and Samantha, but he also needs to know that Maxine was a twin and had a sister. He's not going to believe for one second that that sister is Lola. *That*, I'm afraid is going to take a lot of convincing. But it's the least of our worries. When I left him, I took a box of his with a lot of sentimental shit inside that he will deffo want back. There's a letter to Maxine that she has to read. That's how

Fly

we know everything. It was sealed and we opened it. It was a letter from Jayden's mum to Maxine explaining *everything*. Not even Jayden's read it by the looks of it. We just have to find Maxine, but how in the hell we'll do that is anyone's guess. It'll be like looking for a needle in a haystack. Where the fuck do we even start? She might be dead for all we know. She hasn't been found, so there's still a possibility she's out there. Jayden's always thought she was still alive. We have to go to the police, tell them what we've found out. They might be able to help us, who knows."

"No!"

Jumping out of my skin, near enough hitting the ceiling, I grab Lola and pull her in for a hug, not surprised to see she's also shocked at the urgency in Joni's voice. Stunned as to why he doesn't want Jayden's ass back in jail, my hands calm him down as both Lola and I anxiously wait to hear why he's so agitated.

"The police can't be involved. If they start sniffing around, then you can be bloody certain Jayden will run for the hills, and once he's gone, we'll *never* find him. Don't worry about Maxine, yet. We can deal with her later. Let's deal with Jayden first. Now, what do you want me to do? You know I hate that mother fucker more than anything, and you know I want him to pay for what he's done to you, Jesse, and your beautiful cat."

I don't know, but I've got a funny feeling there's a lot more to why Joni is helping us. My gut tells me. It's like he knows something we don't.

Telling us Jayden will be working later on tonight, the next person we have to get on board is Ricki. Everyone, including Ricki, knows how possessive and jealous Jayden is, but none of them have seen the bruises or the mental scars he's caused up close. Jayden wouldn't dare raise a hand to me or anyone else inside DevO's. Sure, he's given me the death stare too many times to count, but not once has he raised his hand to me when we've come here together. He wouldn't dare expose himself for who he really is. In that respect he's a coward. DevO's will be the perfect place to expose him. I just have to convince Ricki, who thinks the sun shines out of Jayden's arse, that he's an arsehole with a capital A.

Speed dialling Ricki's number, praying to God he's home, nothing can go wrong. Tonight, Jayden has to be made accountable for everything he has done.

Tonight, it's retribution.

Chapter Seventeen
Jayden

If a man hates himself, he takes it out on the woman who loves him.

— *Unknown*

Running up the stairs two at a time, my calves ache, banging through the door, already knowing I'm too late.

Shouting for Jesse to come, the loudness of the noises outside amplify the stony silence of the flat, the hum of the fridge almost as loud as my heart. Where has the bitch gone. Spotting a vodka bottle on the kitchen work surface, making my way to it, I glug back as much as I can.

Crash!

The bottle hits the wall, smashing into a thousand shards as my body shakes with rage, on fire, ready to kill. Fists sore from punching walls, I quickly walk to the bedroom seeing clothes scattered all over the floor. Eyes fixed, looking on in silence at my magazines, they've been thrown all over some clothes on the floor; some ripped up, covering more clothes that have been left in a heap on the wardrobe floor. I'm a volcano, screaming, spewing venom, pulling everything out of the wardrobe until there is nothing left.

My box. Where's is it. "*Where the fuck is my box!*" It has to be here. I told Jesse to never touch it. Ever! She knew that's all I had left of Maxine. It can't be gone. *It can't.*

I'll fucking kill her!

That stupid *cat!* If it wasn't already dead I'd rip out its eyes and cut all its flesh off until there was nothing left but bones. The bitch would still be here, where she belongs if it weren't for that bloody thing. I should've killed the fucking flea-ridden pest long ago.

Kicking clothes out of my way, punching my chest and any wall I can find, a chair I don't even know I've picked up bangs off a wall, roaring, grabbing my helmet and keys, ready to kill. I know exactly where the bitch will be, and it's just lucky I know where her meddling best friend lives.

Slamming the door behind me, I'm down the stairs in seconds ready to annihilate anyone who looks my way. Helmet on, I only have to rev the engine once; riding to Lola's flat like I have fire coming out of the exhaust.

Ten minutes later, parked up across the street, I want those bitches to see me, know that I'm on to them. I want to see them squirm when they look out the window and see me looking up at them.

Hours later, there's been no movement from the flat; I'm not sure if they are even there. They're not dumb. They would've known this is the first place I'd have come. Where the fuck are they. Ready to rip them apart, I'm a lion hunting its prey. I won't let them get away with this. I'll make both of them pay. They're both going to wish they'd never been born.

Ringing a couple of friends, saying I'll pay them to watch the flat for the rest of the day, they report back that there is no one there. Where could they be?

Fly

Riding over, running up the steel stairs two at a time like I'm made of air, I bang the front door of Lola's flat open with my foot until the locks are broken. Whirling through her tiny space, I'm a tornado, grabbing a knife from the kitchen and slashing any photo I can see with it. Striding to her bedroom, rummaging through her drawers, wardrobe, and bedside drawer, I open every box, grabbing some jewellery and pouncing on a stash of drugs I've found in a wooden box. Snorting some cocaine before entering her tiny lounge, there's nothing but crap, throwing everything off tables, seeing a stupid stuffed elephant high on a bookshelf, roaring with rage as I go to grab it just as an ambulance rushes down the Highroad and stops opposite the window. Looking out to the crowd of people surrounding an old man whose collapsed, he's right next to my bike, grabbing my helmet and rushing out. They'll need more than an ambulance when I find the bitches.

Stalking The Orchard for the next two weeks, I can't get anywhere near it. The old Chinese bitch must have Jesse inside, why else would she have suddenly hired two massive bodyguards. Hell, Gonzo, her usual bouncer, would've put me off, alone. I've always hated him and his smarmy face.

Girls start turning up for work in police cars, guessing the old bitch must have told them some bullshit story. The pigs will definitely be getting freebies for this one. I should've guessed. They're all corrupt.

If the cops are helping, then Jesse won't be in there. I've been around the block enough times to know that I'm barking up the wrong tree.

I have to find her.
I have to find my box.

. . .

Not getting anywhere fast, how the hell am I going to get my box back? Blood boiling, all I think about is Maxine, her unopened letter, my photos, money, cap, souvenir eye, and fang. How will I find my beloved sister without it all?

Why didn't I lock the door when I left?

Why the fuck didn't I lock the door?

I have to find a way to lure Jesse back. I'll lure her back, and then I'll kill her. I'll kill the bitch with my own two hands, and then I'll kill Lola, too. I'll kill them both.

Jesse will come back. She always does. Always. I should've got rid of her months ago. She's turned out like all the rest. I thought she'd be different. I thought I'd chosen the right one, but she's turned out more useless than my mother. She's more useless than my pathetic excuse of a mother ever was.

When I get to work tonight, I'll act like everything is fine. I'll go up to that geek DJ and corner him and ask if he's seen her. He's always had a soft spot for Jesse so I'll know if he's helping her just by his reaction. If he's helping her, I'll kill him. I'll kill anyone who is helping her. I'll find the bitch if it's the last thing I do.

Chapter Eighteen
Jesse

You never realise how strong you are, until being strong is the only choice you have.

— Bob Marley

Arriving at his office approximately fifteen minutes after our call, Ricki asks what the hell is going on, looking at me with doubtful eyes when I tell him how living with Jayden for the last two years has nearly killed me. It's only when I tell him about Samantha that his ears prick up. He knows how much I loved her, and having to relive the day she died is bringing back the torture of not having her here. His dark-brown eyes glistening with tears, he simply can't believe Jayden could hurt a fly, let alone kill a cat! Reminiscing back to when he knew Jayden's father, he says he didn't once hear him say anything bad about his son.

"If Jayden is as evil as you say, then Jimmy would've told me. We were good friends. I knew him for years. He used to come here sometimes, with friends of his. He was always talking about his boy and wife with nothing but love. Jayden can't be his. Jimmy was so gentle, so charming. He'd be turning in his grave if he knew what was going on."

Eyes locked with Ricki's; my stare tells him I'm not making it up. Why would I. Why would I have come all the way down here, phoned him and asked him to come to his office if I was making it all up. He knows it has to be true. If it weren't for the box and finding Maxine's letter, or finding out Jayden is related in some way to Lola and I, then I wouldn't be here, putting mine and everyone else's lives at risk.

"We have to tell Jayden about his sister's letter, Ricki. You know how much he loved her, *still* loves her. Maxine ran from the house trying to protect her mother from him. It all makes sense now why Jayden hates women so much. His mother even said in the letter that she knew Jayden, her own son, would kill her one day. Maybe that's why she died. Her body was completely incinerated. The bastard could've easily killed her and made it look like an accident. The letter, Ricki. The letter said both Jayden and his father were monsters. Believe me, the apple has definitely not fallen far from the tree where's Jayden's concerned. Whatever you think you know about Jayden's father, isn't true. He was as evil as his son. Where do you think Jayden got it from? I wish it was all a nightmare I'd be waking up from soon, but it's not. Jayden has to be told that Maxine has a twin, a blood sister. He's not going to believe it's Lola. Who would? No-one, would've, could've predicted that! We have to get him to listen before he kills us."

Backing down, Ricki agrees to letting us confront Jayden in the club later on tonight. I think in his heart he knows that what I'm saying is true. He's seen for himself just how easy Jayden can turn. Even though he's never seen him physically touch me, he's seen the bruises and the way I jump when Jayden speaks to me. He's seen Jayden chatting up women, and, I'm sure he's seen him leave with them, too. Ricki knows more than he's letting on.

"Ok, you can use the club for what you need tonight, but, there is one proviso. If he's as dangerous as you say, then people must be protected. There will be bodyguards incognito to jump in if needed."

Agreeing to everything he wants; nothing can go wrong.

Joni, who's been listening from the back, is unusually quiet. After hearing everything, he's not reacting the way I would've expected. I can see him seething on the inside, but he's keeping it together, like a dormant volcano ready to erupt. I can feel it. There's something he's not saying. He's not as excited as I would have expected him to be to see Jayden finally getting his comeuppance. Why? He absolutely *hates* Jayden. I don't know if I'm being paranoid, but I think he has something up his sleeve. God, I hope I'm wrong.

Suddenly butting in with an idea she's had, Lola breaks the silence, distracting my thoughts.

"I'll phone Tiffany to keep a lookout on the streets for Jayden or anyone he might've paid to look for us. She won't tell the girls anything, so don't worry. I know they all trust her."

Looking towards Joni, seeing him recognise his sister's name, he growls at Lola who ignores him. Not wanting anything to distract from what's going on, I quickly jump in, diverting the conversation to Roy.

"What about Roy? He won't be happy about it. She's his girl, Lola. He won't want Tiffany put in any unnecessary danger. We have to tell him first to see if he's ok with it."

Quickly ringing Roy, he's a little apprehensive at first, but knows Tiffany could be a big help, especially as she is practically queen of the streets and knows a lot of people.

Telling us he'll hire two more bodyguards and put them incognito, we later hear they aren't happy that Roy's told them to dress in women's clothes. He says it's to make them look less conspicuous, but Tiffany tells us they stick out like two sore thumbs. The girls on the street think it's the funniest thing they've seen in ages, telling Tiffany to thank Roy for the laughs.

The bodyguards aren't impressed.

. . .

Late afternoon, still in Ricki's office, Lola, Joni, and myself discuss what the plan of attack will be later on when Jayden arrives. Joni speaks first.

"We definitely can't tell Greg. He'll spoil everything, you know what a bigmouth he is."

Even though I know Joni is right, I feel I have to stick up for Greg who isn't here to defend himself.

"Don't be like that, Joni. Greg can be a little bit annoying, but he has a heart of gold. Lola, I know you have a 'strained' relationship with him, but you've got to suck it up tonight and make sure he doesn't cotton on to anything. Please, do it for me."

Lola's slitted eyes kill me on the spot. Hand on her hips, she's back to normal. It didn't take her long.

"Alright! Don't hold back, freak! I'll try my best, but you know what he's like with me. I don't know why the geek hates me so much. It's not like I even knew him before I came to the city. He probably secretly likes me. It's the same with all the nerds."

Ricki, unusually, speaks up.

"Now, Lola, tonight is not about you. Don't worry, I'll make sure you get a few drinks free for helping out. Just make sure you don't go to Jayden's part of the bar. You need to stay out of sight for as long as possible. If he sees you, you'll blow the cover for everyone; he'll know Jesse is here."

Winking, giving Lola his sexiest devilish grin, she's not having any of it.

"Oh, Ricki, you so know I will. That creep has to pay for what he did to Jesse, and Samantha. I'm just looking forward to watching him squirm. Thank God I'm *not* related to him. Poor Maxine living with him for all those years. He's an arsehole. My dad's coming later. I've told him I have some exciting news to tell him. He has to know about Gail, Maxine, and Jesse before my mother finds out. She'll freak when she hears that I'm Maxine's twin, and that Jesse's my cousin. I'll remind her of the time she took me to Jesse's house to look for her. She could tell I was worried, but that bitch was only interested in getting to her nail appointment on time. She couldn't have cared less that my best friend had gone missing, that the creep who answered the door had been touching Jesse up for months. I *hate* her! I'd love to be a fly on the wall when Dad tells her I've found not only my birth mother, but a twin sister, too. If only it hadn't been *her* who'd adopted me."

Running to Lola and hugging her, I'm surprised at how emotional she is, which is making me emotional. I love her, but am panicking at what she has planned. Nothing can go wrong. I know what she's doing is out of love, but I don't want her to ruin everything.

"Come on, Lola. What's important tonight is making sure Jayden hears and listens to us before we get killed. You have a twin who we have to find, don't you? I know your mum was a bitch, is still a bitch, and I love you for checking up on me back then, but telling your dad to come tonight might not be the best decision. You need to focus on what we have to do. After tonight, you can go for it and tell him everything. Nothing can go wrong. I really don't think telling your dad you're related to a psycho who's been in prison and possibly killed his mother, is the right thing to do. Please, think about it?"

Looking towards Ricki and Joni for support, they're both staring, in shock, shaking their heads, watching as Lola breaks from my hold. I don't think she's having any of it.

"*Bull*, it isn't. I *need* my dad, Jesse. I don't know how Jayden's going to react when he finds out I'm Maxine's twin. I want my dad there, ok? Jayden has to pay for what he's done to you, and Samantha. His days of being a prick are over. He's going to pay."

"Ok, I get it, Lola. Why are you so angry, though? I mean, I know you're pissed off hearing what he's done to me and Samantha, but why are *you* so angry? What's he done to you to make you like this?"

I know Lola like the back of my hand. There's something she's not telling me; I have to know what it is before we go on. Eyeballing her until she cracks, I'm not prepared for what she's about to say.

"Ok, you want to hear it? *I slept with the bastard before you met him.* I was never going to tell you, but it's the right thing to do considering the circumstances. It was only the once. After he clapped eyes on you it was sayonara to me. He only used me to get to you. I'm sorry, Jesse. Please, forgive me. It's all so fucked up now that we know the truth. When he finds out I'm Maxine's twin he's going to freak out about the night we ... *did* it. How was I to know this was going to happen? Thank God the bastard isn't a blood brother. That would have made it even more revolting than it already is."

Disbelief, anger, horror. I don't quite know what to do. It all makes so much sense. Now I know why Jayden hated me going out with her, or for that matter, being anywhere near her. It wasn't because he loved me and wanted me all to himself. It was because of what had happened between them. I can't say I'm not surprised. Lola's done this to me my whole life, and the fact she didn't tell me about Jayden, proves she must have felt something for him. She'd usually have rubbed it right in my face, like she did with Jim. Right now, I want to kill her. I want to hurt her, rip her apart for deciding to tell me now. Of all the times. Ready to explode, Joni comes close, feeling his strong arms around me as he glares at Lola. Even Ricki is glaring at her, sure he's thinking the same thing as Joni. How could anyone be so vindictive, so cruel? Especially to their best friend. It's unthinkable. This is the lowest she's ever stooped, unsure of whether I can even talk to her. Joni, thank God, defuses the tension.

"Come on, Jesse. Lola didn't know who he was back then, and if she says it was before Jayden met you, then he was fair game. She knows she *should've* told you she knew him, but what's the point of going over it, now."

Glaring Lola's way, his gritted teeth continue to speak while her remorseful eyes look to the floor.

"He has to pay for everything he's done to everyone, *including* Lola. You girls are family, now, so you have to try to let it go. You have to stay focused on what you both have to do. Remember? Come on, hug it out. Don't let that prick come between you two. Not him. Don't you think he's done enough damage to everyone?"

I don't want to hug or do anything with Lola, but hating each other at this moment in time isn't going to get us anywhere. Lola did look after me for weeks, and she was the one who found me the day I ran, so I have to think of that and find a way through the anger. For now, I'll forgive her, but I won't forget. This will be the last time she ever does this to me, *ever*. Pulling her to me, hugging, crying together, she's a blubbing mess which tells me she really is sorry for what she's done. Never in our lives has she been so emotional like this over a guy.

Ricki and Joni join in, embracing us in a circle, none of us saying anything. Two minutes later, wiping our eyes and patting each other down, we all sit, finalising plans for the night.

Deciding last minute to dress in the men's wigs and clothes we used to meet Sharon, we drive back to Roy's in silence, going separate ways when we arrive. Arranging to meet in the kitchen in ten minutes, Sharon is already there waiting for us. Sensing the tension between us, her concerned face says nothing. I'm guessing Ricki has rung her and told her. She knows not to say anything.

Looking from one face to the other as we tell her the plan for the night, she tells us she's coming to the club, too, asking if we have a spare wig.

"I want to see that creep get what he deserves. You are family, now. Both of you. Remember that. I must be there to look after you. Gail would want that. Gail would want her daughter and niece protected, okay?"

Hugging Sharon and leaving Lola to help her dress, I quickly run up to my room and walk over to the box beside my bed. Raising it up to my lips, kissing Samantha's picture for luck, I stroke her beautiful face with my fingers wishing so much she was still here with me. I miss her so much, it hurts. I don't even taste the saltiness of my tears until I place Samantha's picture to my forehead, swearing I hear her meowing.

"Tonight, my darling, I'll get him back for you. I'll make sure the bastard pays for what he did to you. He will pay."

Setting the box back down on the table, running back to the kitchen just as Sharon is helping secure Gail's necklace around Lola's neck, I grab my own necklace, kissing the centre, nodding to them both.

"Right, let's go do this. Let's go get the fucker."

Chapter Nineteen

Remember, you may choose your sin, but you cannot choose the consequences.

— Jenny Sanford

You could cut the tension in the car with a knife. Passing motorbike after motorbike, constantly thinking every single one is Jayden, sweat drips from my forehead, thankful when we finally arrive at the club a good two hours before anyone else is due to start work. Roy's already jumped out and phoning Ricki from a phone box across the street as we exit the car, fanning ourselves as we wait for him to come down and let us in. Seeing him walking towards the door, he opens it, unable to hold in how he feels, trying not to laugh, coughing into his hand.

"Aren't you *all* looking lovely tonight, ladies? Um, especially you, Roy."

Shifting his shoulder-length orange wig, smiling sarcastically, hunching his shoulders, Roy is in no mood for jokes.

"Oh, be quiet. It's all we had. Do you know how bloody hot these things are to wear? If I could, I'd go back and change into something else, but it's too late. We're here now."

Following Ricki and the others up to his office, I eye up the CCTV, wondering why Roy phoned. Surely Ricki would've seen us? Watching Roy's driver park up across the street at the same time looking out for any signs of Jayden or anyone else he might've hired to search for us, I'm paranoid and scared our disguises aren't good enough.

Ricki, not his usual upbeat and suave self, is smoking coffin nail after coffin nail, pacing up and down his office, looking at the cameras above with anxious eyes. Sharon, who is also nervous, holds Jayden's box close to her chest as she joins him; very soon the office looks like there's a barbecue being cooked indoors. Coughing, waving the smoke from my face, it's revolting and making my eyes sting, which isn't making it easy to watch the cameras.

"Bloody hell, you two. Give our lungs and eyes a break, will you, and smoke your coffin nails somewhere else."

Puffing her cigarette, looking through the haze, Sharon places the box on a table and stares at me with eyes so soft, you'd swear she was my mother. No-one else but me knows how anxious she is. For as long as I've known her she's been able to mask how she feels, but tonight, I can tell just by the amount she's smoking, and her incessant pacing, that she's terrified of seeing Jayden, backing up what I think almost straight away.

"Sorry, Jesse. I'm too nervous to see your nasty boyfriend. You know I don't like him, and I don't know what will happen tonight if he sees you and his box. It's so dangerous. I don't want anything to happen to you, or Lola. I'm praying to my beautiful friend Gail, that tonight she will help us. She won't want anything bad happening to her girls."

Blessing herself, flinging off her red wig and throwing it across the room, she wipes her forehead before lighting another long cigarette. Following her eyes to Ricki, he is on the phone, nodding to

Fly

whoever is speaking to him. Returning the receiver, looking at us with trepidation, I'm already worried.

"That was Joni. He says he's going to be a bit late."

Just by the way his eyes scan us one by one, I know that he thinks Joni is up to something. His voice confirms I'm right.

"Joni's *never* late. Not once in all the time he's worked here, has he ever been late. I don't know, but I don't have a good feeling about this."

Staring at each other, no one says what they are thinking, jumping in unison as a loud boom comes from inside the club. Walking slowly to the window, spying Greg below in his booth, he is none the wiser that we're watching him from above as he tests the microphones and speakers, playing *'You Oughta Know'* by *Alanis Morrisette* at full blast, bopping about in his booth. His dark curly hair jumps up and down as he sings along, pointing to the walls. Looking at each other, shaking our heads, we all try not to laugh at his choice of song. It's like he has a sixth sense that something bad is going to happen.

An hour later, and still no sign of Joni, I'm really starting to worry. What is he doing? He knew what the plan was. When he left this afternoon, he was excited to see Jayden get his retribution. Where is he? He won't want to miss it.

Thankfully, Sharon has helped Ricki organise someone else for the door at short notice. Nick, one of her big bouncers from The Orchard who is the size of an ox, stands at the entrance, ready to let people in.

Now that everyone is in place, all we can do is wait for Jayden to appear, and we don't have very long to wait.

Arriving bang on nine o'clock, I admit, it's strange seeing him again. Heart racing, my head feels dizzy; I'm sweating, terrified he'll see me and come and finish me off. Half of me wants to run to him and put my arms around his neck and hug him, the other half wants to kill him for what he did to my Samantha, to me. I know I shouldn't, but I still have feelings for him, which I hate myself for. They're so hard for me to control. It's like my heart and head are out of sync.

My stomach is in knots.

Ducking down, watching Jayden from above as he walks in the door and says hi to the new doorman, I know he's suspicious. I'd know his body language anywhere; the way he's scanning Nick's huge body with slitted eyes, tells me he's suspicious as hell. Glancing over his shoulder, Jayden slowly walks up the steps and suddenly stops and yells back to Nick asking where Joni is. Shrugging his shoulders when Nick tells him he doesn't have a clue, Nick further explains he was called in at short notice, which Jayden seems satisfied with, saluting him and continuing up the steps to the door at the top. Racing to the other side of Ricki's office, we all watch as Jayden steps through the door and shouts to someone at the bar that he's going up to talk to Ricki for five minutes. Sharon shrieks, stumbling her words.

"You quickly go! *Ricki!* Before Jayden sees us. He cannot see Jesse, or Lola. It's too dangerous. He's a madman. *Quick!*"

Walking as fast as light, I've never seen Ricki move so quick. Heart thumping in my head, I crouch, watching him at the door, sweating in unison with him as he prepares to go out and face Jayden. I'm not sure, but I think Ricki's gone green, praying he doesn't crumble and spoil the plan. It can't all go tits up, now. Sshhing us with his fingers, he slowly opens the door and slips out, greeting Jayden half way down the stairs.

Jayden's voice, metres from me, takes me back to the last time we were together, remembering the crack as Samantha's body hit the wall. Head on fire, closing my eyes, visualising hurting him, I want to go out and kill him, make him suffer in the worst way.

What I would do to have Samantha here with me now.

Lola suddenly comes close, giving me a hug. She must feel my anxiety at being near Jayden again and, I guess, she's just as anxious knowing how she felt about him. Whispering, "don't worry Jesse,

Fly

we've got this," I'm glad she's with me, even though she did sleep with him.

For all these years I've thought I was the more insecure one out of the two of us, her having any man she wanted at the flick of her head. After hearing she slept with Jayden, and how he rejected her for me, I realise she's way more insecure than I'll ever be.

Squeezing her hand, breathing out with relief as Ricki and Jayden start to walk down the stairs into the club, we rush to the window and all look out, watching with x-ray eyes the activity below before it opens.

A bartender is lining up glasses fresh out of the dishwasher while another makes sure all the bottles in the fridge are replenished. Girls in white, short-sleeved shirts, and short, black skirts, wrap aprons around their waists, ready for taking money and collecting tips.

Walking up to a busty brunette, Jayden whispers in her ear, squeezes her bum and looks into her eyes with lust.

Overcome with jealousy, I want to jump through the window and tear her apart, tear Jayden apart. He's moved on so quickly. There's not a sign of remorse for what's happened with me, with Samantha.

Holding me back, Lola grabs my wrist, hard, rubbing my scars, staring into my face with wide eyes.

"Don't let him get to you. He's a *prick*. Remember why we're here, Jesse. He hurt you, and Samantha. You better believe he's hurt others, too, and is doing exactly the same to some poor girl as we speak. Just thank God you're out of it, now. Remember, you're out of it. You don't want to go back there, *ever!* He's someone else's problem, now, so try and focus on what we have to do. Please. After tonight, you don't ever have to see him again. I promise. You won't ever have to see that prick again."

Hugging her, crying, I don't know how to feel. I didn't think my feelings would still be so strong. It's torture seeing him with someone else. It's torture imagining he is touching her, loving her, kissing her in places he used to kiss me.

Wiping my eyes, trying to control myself from doing something stupid, I continue watching the activity below. Greg is eyeing Jayden up, looking at him with hate. I know how he feels. Playing *'Highway to Hell,'* staring at Jayden and laughing, the waitresses sexily dance as Jayden walks off tapping each of their chins like they are his harem.

I hate him. I hate him. I hate them all.

Has he been doing this the whole time? Has Joni been right all along? Joni! Where is he? I need him here.

Walking towards Greg, Jayden suddenly grabs him by the throat, yelling into his face with hate. We can't hear what he's saying, but we're all worried for Greg's safety, seeing his head shake from side to side, both arms up in surrender. Two bartenders run to Greg's booth, each taking Jayden by an arm, escorting him to the bar until he's calmed down.

What the hell was that?

Poor Greg. What the hell has Jayden got against him. He's done absolutely nothing to him.

Downstairs, Ricki looks on, approaching Jayden to ask if everything is alright, looking up towards us with worry as Jayden answers him. Walking over towards Greg and patting him on the back, Ricki makes sure he is ok before heading back to the front door. The stress is showing, rubbing his chiselled chin, looking towards us again with hands in prayer before he parks himself by the door.

Please let him get through tonight. Please, let all of us get through tonight. Please God, nothing can go wrong.

Chapter Twenty

Audiences like to see the bad guy get their comeuppance.

— *Charles Bronson*

People start arriving, and soon the club fills up. Ricki stays downstairs by the door handing out poker chips to everyone for a free drink.

Whispering to each other in Ricki's office, I'm still livid with how Jayden is acting, hardly hearing what anyone is saying. Distracting how I feel with images of Samantha, suddenly I'm thinking about Joni, too. I want to see him and tell him I'm sorry for not believing him. I need Joni here to stop me doing something stupid. I'm desperately worried that something bad has happened to him. Where is he.

A sharp elbow in the ribs by Lola brings me back. Nodding, pointing to the floor below, her eyes are wide.

"Fuck me, Jesse. Look at the size of that bloke. He's bloody mahoooosive!"

Following her finger, I don't believe what I'm seeing. It can't be *him*. Frozen, I can't move; I think I'm going to pass out.

"What is it, Jesse? Are you alright? Speak to me."

Pointing to the man, I can hardly talk. Not in a million years did I think I'd ever see him again.

"I-I-I-I ..."

"What, Jesse! What's wrong?"

I-i-i-it's that creepy man. The officer I told you about, remember? The car I nearly got into, outside the train station the night my mother flung me out. I'd recognise that creepy clown grin anywhere. What the hell is he doing here? I've never seen him here before. What's he doing here? What the fuck is he doing here tonight? He can't spoil anything. He can't."

"Far out, Jesse. Do you think he's working for Jayden? It's too much of a coincidence he's turned up here tonight. Why? Why is he here tonight? He looks like a major creep. There's deffo something shifty going on with him. He's fricking massive. Maybe Ricki, or Roy hired him."

"God knows. Look, he's going to sit at the back, in the corner where no one can see him. He's a dodgy bastard. I'll ask Ricki about him when he comes up. Please God he doesn't know him."

Watching the creepy guy slither around a corner, he sits in the dark, watching everyone as the club fills with more people. Jayden hasn't seen him, too busy serving people at the bar. Greg is busy playing his favourite song telling everyone to 'masturbate,' instead of celebrate. I wish he'd stop doing that, it's getting bloody boring.

Hearing a commotion from the front entrance, we all run to the other side of the office to see what's happening. Watching out the window overlooking the entrance to the club, we see Joni's arrived. But he's not alone. Running up the stairs two at a time, his face is thunder, holding the doors at the top open for whoever he's brought. Who is it?

"What the hell is Joni doing, Jesse? Who the fuck has he brought? He didn't tell us about this. This is probably why he's late. He's going to ruin everything. *Everything!* He better not ruin it or I'll flipping kill him."

Fly

Looking at me, green in the face, I know how Lola feels, because I feel it, too. Sharon lights another cigarette and Roy, unusually joins her, quickly grabbing Lola's arm and guiding her through the smoke to the window overlooking the club. Ricki's trying to restrain Joni at the door, but has no chance against him. He's yelling, flinging Ricki off, looking straight towards the bar for Jayden. Clutching the hand of his companion, Joni strides forward like a bull charging towards a red flag.

He can't be doing this.

Please, God, let me be hallucinating.

This wasn't the plan.

From the back of the club, the huge officer stands, staring, silent, fixated on whoever Joni has brought.

Is he working for Joni?

Looking up, Jayden's still none the wiser, smiling to a customer he's preparing a drink for. Looking towards the commotion, he suddenly sees Joni, dropping the glass, not even flinching when it smashes all over the bar. Turning as white as a ghost, Jayden stares at the person Joni has brought and, mouth agape, like the air has been sucked out of the room and all he stands in is a vacuum, it looks like he might pass out.

Who the hell has Joni brought?

What the hell is going on?

We have to get down there.

We have to get down there, now!

Chapter Twenty-One
Jesse

The shock of any trauma, I think, changes your life.

— Alex Lifeson

Running down the stairs two at a time, Lola and I race through the club to the bar, crouching behind two tall men. My blonde wig nearly falls off, scratching my scalp, repositioning it just as Jayden jumps over the bar and stands in front of Joni and the mystery woman he has brought.

I want to see her.

Who is she?

Bending my head to get a good look at her, the man I'm behind looks around and down giving me a filthy look. Ignoring him, looking up to the lights still twirling above, they are casting patterns on the mystery woman's face and body, gasping when I see her scarred skin. Nudging Lola to see if she's seen, too, she's already staring at me, mouth wide open, pointing to different places on her face. Whispering in my ear, she sounds scared.

Fly

"Who the hell is she, Jesse? She looks like she's just stepped off a horror movie. It's awful. I'm scared. What if whoever did this to her is in here, watching?"

I don't tell her I'm scared, too. I haven't even given it a thought that the person who might've done that could be in here. Shivering all over, someone touches me from behind making me jump. Snapping my head to see who it is, Sharon and Roy are behind me, raising my eyes and telling them to shh, but they start whispering in our ears.

"Who is girl? Why did Joni bring her? I'm getting too confused."

Turning to Sharon, my eyes tell her to shut up, but Roy suddenly butts in, making me angrier.

"Whoever she is, something bad happened to her. Look at all those scars. That poor girl. I need to know if my Tiffany is safe. I'm going to get her. I'll be right back. Don't do anything."

Watching Roy run off, I grasp Sharon and bring her to my side, crouching behind more people, watching Jayden, who is still staring at the mystery woman in shock. I don't know what the fuck is going on. Watching Jayden's lips, I just make out what he mouths above the music.

"M-m-m-Maxine? Max? Is it you? Is it really you?"

Have I seen properly? Unblinking, looking towards Lola, mouthing Maxine to her, she's turned green again. I don't think she, or any of us, were expecting to see or meet Maxine tonight. Pointing to Maxine and hunching her shoulders, we shake our heads not knowing what to do. Could it be her? Could it really be Maxine, her twin?

Long, straight hair as black as night frames a face the same oval shape as Lola's, and through the light, her dark-blue almond eyes look on hauntedly at Jayden, who is still staring straight at her tiny trembling body. She looks like a frightened bird. Flinching at the flicker of recognition between herself and her brother, she takes something from behind her back and places it on her head.

Jayden's face freezes.

M.A. McNally

My eyes freeze.
Lola's eyes freeze.
It can't be.
How in God's name did she get it?

Chapter Twenty-Two

You cannot defeat your enemies until you know who they are.

— Anthony Horowitz

Greg, sensing that something important is happening, suddenly dulls the music as Joni quickly looks around for someone or something, me crouching down low, pushing Lola and Sharon down with me as the people in front turn around and look down, questioning us with their eyes. Smiling up to them coyly, I pretend to pick something up from the floor and they turn back uninterested in what I'm doing to watch the exchange between Joni and Jayden. This is unreal, having to pinch myself to believe it's really happening. Jayden's voice is all I hear.

"Maxine? My sister. Is it you? Dad's cap. How did you get Dad's cap? That was in my box. Did *you* take my box? How? It doesn't make any sense. How the hell could you have known about my box? Where is it? *Where's my box?* I've always known you were alive. I never stopped looking for you. *Never.* I knew in my heart that you'd come back. My sister."

Running to embrace her, Joni steps forward, stopping Jayden by forming a barrier with his arm between brother and sister.

Eyes wild, pulsing out of their sockets like they have a heart, Jayden stares up into Joni's face like he wants to kill him.

He's about to turn, and Joni doesn't have a clue.

Snarling into Joni's face, Jayden forms his left hand into a fist, shaking from his feet right through to his head, screaming at him through gritted teeth.

"*Joni*. What the fuck are you doing? Get the fuck away from my sister. Maxine? Get away from him. Get away from him, *now!* How do you even know him? Maxine! *What the fuck is going on?*"

Using Joni as her shield, Maxine screams as Jayden springs forward to embrace her making her cap fall off her head to the floor. Rugby tackling Jayden, Joni throws him down the stairs onto the dance floor as everyone follows.

Snatching the cap off the floor before anyone sees, I quickly follow everyone else to the dance floor, finding Lola and Sharon glued to what's going on.

On top of Jayden, Joni's ripping him apart with his fists, legs, teeth; poor Maxine is screaming from behind as people form a circle around the scene.

Watching the two enemies near enough killing each other, Lola whispers in my ear from behind.

"What the hell is going on? And where is Ricki? Why isn't he stopping this? I thought he had security."

"Shhh, I don't know! I'm asking myself the same bloody question. It looks like Ricki's done a runner. Let's pray to God I'm wrong and he shows up before they bloody kill each other."

Shaking her head, Lola doesn't look convinced.

"Did you know about Joni and Maxine? How can she be with him? Everyone, including her brother thought she was dead. I'm so confused, Jesse. How in the hell are we going to confront Jayden, now? Joni's ruined everything."

Fly

Shrugging my shoulders and embracing her, I try my best to comfort her.

"We can't do anything about it now, Lola. Just wait. We'll hopefully get our chance once someone stops them fighting."

Quickly following the screaming, Jayden and Joni kick, punch, and slap each other anywhere they can, the people surrounding them shouting loudly, enjoying the battle as they urge them on like they're watching gladiators in a ring. I've never seen anything like it. Two men beside me dressed in identical *Siouxsie & the Banshees* t-shirts, scream, bumping into me as they watch the display. I'm not prepared for how I react, shoving one of them off me with force, expecting he's going to hit me. Giving me the evils sideways, he moves forward looking at me like I'm some sort of nutcase.

Fuck, the way I feel at the moment, he could be right.

I'm going crazy trying to put two and two together and coming up with a big fat nothing. I'm in utter disbelief that Joni would, could be involved in this. Not my Joni. Not my soft spoken, big teddy bear Joni who wouldn't even hurt a fly. How in God's name does he even know Maxine? Is she the mysterious new love he's never wanted anyone to meet? She has to be. She has to be the reason he's been acting so cagey. He must've known all along he was going to do this and I'm more than a little pissed off he kept something so important from us. Hopefully, tonight we'll get some answers.

Suddenly, without warning, Joni grabs Jayden up off the floor and holds both his arms behind his back as Jayden tries in vain to kick him from behind. Covered in blood, Jayden's shirt, nose, and eyes look like he's done ten rounds in a boxing ring. He may as well have. He doesn't stand a chance against Joni, who looks like he only has one thing on his mind. Waiting for Joni to speak, the tension in the air could be cut with a knife.

Behind them Maxine cries, frantically looking around the floor. I know what she's looking for because I have it in my hand, looking down towards the cap as Lola spots it, gesturing to her to zip it before she gives me away.

Jumping when Jayden yells, we both turn, seeing Maxine's still looking at the floor, confused, crying like a baby searching for its mother. I want to run to her, hug her, let her know I have what she seeks. I want to tell her she is safe but just as I go to step forward, Lola pushes me back, shaking her head. Turning quickly to Joni, we listen as he starts to speak.

"Yeah, you bastard. I know your sister. And you wanna know how? You remember the night she was running from *you*? Remember? You were beating your mother, again. I bet you killed her. I bet it was *your* fault your mother died."

Trying to kick Joni from behind, Jayden winces as Joni whacks his leg, making him nearly fall. Screaming into the side of Jayden's face, Joni's hatred for him is obvious; I'm now very worried for Jayden's safety, not entirely sure Joni isn't going to kill him. Joni's spit hits Jayden's face as he continues to snarl into it.

"She wouldn't have had to run if it weren't for *you*. I found her that night, on the road, left for dead. Whoever took her left her in the woods, under some filthy rotten leaves after he stabbed her like a pin cushion and stubbed out his cigarette on her flesh."

The crowd gasps in unison, and Lola and I stare at each other in horror as Joni continues.

"Only God knows how she had the strength to walk up that hill, near death, to find someone to help her. She wouldn't have had to do that if she hadn't been running from *you*! You bastard. It was your fault. *Yours!* If I hadn't found her, what do you think would've happened? What do you think would've happened if the prick had come back to finish her off? You're so lucky I haven't finished *you* off for what you did to your mother for all those years. The only reason I haven't is because Maxine's begged me not to. She doesn't want you dead for some reason. She wants *you* to find the monster who left her for dead, and she wants you to help me kill him. You owe her. You owe her that much, you prick. *Au na vakamatei iko!*"

Growling at Joni, Jayden looks towards Maxine, asking her through gritted teeth.

Fly

"He pono tēnei? *He pono?*"

Stepping forward, squeezing Joni's arm, Maxine whispers in his ear, and just like that, Jayden is released from his grasp. Standing next to Maxine, Jayden's bloodied face cries to be near his sister; the crowds murmur, some even laughing at the pathetic scene. All I want to do is run to him and put my arms around him and hug him.

This is his softer side, the one I love. I know his sister will come to no harm.

Maxine begins speaking as Ricki suddenly appears, standing to the side of Joni with his security guards in tow, ready to jump in if needed. Roy, who is behind Ricki, holds onto a woman who must be Tiffany. She has her arm wrapped around his shoulder; her face as fearful as everyone else's in the room. Poking me in the ribs, Lola points over to them, waving, confirming what I've just thought.

"There's Ricki! And Roy, and Tiffany. She looks scared."

Grabbing her hand, yanking it down, I give her my best death glare, telling her to shut up.

"Shh, you'll get us bloody seen. Zip it!"

If looks could kill, I'd definitely be dead. Pursing her lips, Lola defiantly waves at Tiffany who's giving her dirty looks. Lola's obviously forgotten she's dressed in men's clothes, and wearing a wig. She never bloody listens. Nudging her to stop and watch, we look on as Maxine takes Jayden's hand. She seems calmer, less anxious than before.

Stepping back, giving them the space they need, people are shouting at Jayden calling him a prick and loser. He's only a few feet from me, swearing I can smell his favourite Kouros aftershave. I'm terrified and happy at the same time not knowing what to do. Luckily, I don't have to wait long, watching as he squeezes Maxine's hand and nods, speaking in the softest voice I've ever heard.

"Go on, my sister. Talk."

Smiling at him, the noise suddenly dims; Maxine begins to speak.

"Kei te tika. It's true, my brother. Joni found me nearly dead. I don't know how many times I was stabbed. I think I stopped counting after the blade hit me seven, eight, nine times. I begged Joni not to take me to the hospital. I did it to save you, Jayden. I knew the police would think you'd done it. I didn't want you to take the rap for something you hadn't done. I should've let Joni, though. I should've let him do it. All the times you beat our mother. I should've let you suffer. I should've kept our mother safe, but I was too weak. I didn't have the strength. I didn't tell Joni about you being my brother for a long time. When he found out, it took every last bit of strength I had to stop him going to the police. The only reason he didn't do that was for me."

"Max, I'm so sorry. You know I'm sorry for everything. You know I am. I don't want to lose you, again. Please, forgive me."

"I know you are, brother. But you need to know how much I hated you. I hated you for hurting our mother, for making me run that night, for making me jump into that maniac's car. I thought I was safe. He had a uniform on. I thank God it was Joni who found me, and not that maniac coming back to finish me off. Without Joni I'd be dead. You owe it to him for me being alive. He took me back to his flat, sewed my skin together with a needle and cotton, and nursed me back to health. His doctor training was what saved me. I was so lucky. I could look a lot worse than I do now. Joni took care of me until I was strong enough to talk. I told him about you, about what you used to do to our mother, and asked him to drive me to our house to find her, but when we got there, both our house and Mother were gone. The neighbours' told me what happened, but I'm sure you killed her. I've heard you've been searching for me for years, but I don't know why. Do you think I wanted you to find me? Really? *No!* I didn't, but now I don't have a choice. There are things that have been discovered that you need to know."

This is unreal.

Is it even happening?

Looking sideways at Lola, she's shaking her head from side-to-side, crying. I know why. This is the first time she's seen, heard her sister, her twin.

Suddenly hearing our names, Maxine's shouting for us in the

Fly

crowd as people look around murmuring, parting where we stand, ruining our cover. Cowering, taking off our wigs, Jayden spots us, growling. Ignoring him and looking towards Maxine, her arms ask us to come.

"Jesse, Lola. It's time."

Stepping forward, standing in front of Jayden, Joni, and Maxine, there's a commotion behind and everyone looks around to see Sharon running forward with something in her hand.

"Jesse, Lola, you forgot your box. I run upstairs and get it for you."

Handing me the box, Sharon steps back, hiding behind a tall man, glaring at Jayden who tries to grab it from me.

Roaring from the back, the crowd parts again as the huge officer we saw earlier steps forward and grabs Jayden around the throat. There's something glistening in his right hand, screaming when I realise what it is. The noise around me dims, hearing only my screaming as the blade punctures Jayden's skin, blood pouring from his side as he steps forward and falls to the floor.

"No!"

Chapter Twenty-Three

I can't believe that I still miss you after everything that we went through.

— *Unknown*

Running to Jayden with a voice I don't recognise, I crouch down, flinging the box down before trying to stop the stream of blood from his side with my hand. Maxine's screaming beside me, yelling for help when suddenly the officer grabs her around the throat and the same knife, covered in Jayden's blood, is positioned on her neck. Backing away with her in tow, we all listen in horror.

"*Shut up!* If you don't stop screaming, I'll kill you, *again!* Don't anyone come near her, or I swear, she's dead."

Bending down and rubbing his cheek to Maxine's like he loves her, what the hell is going on? Does he love her? Joni's growling, ready to kill him. Maxine looks on in terror as the officer starts to speak.

"My love. I only came in tonight to see what the place was like. I can't believe it's you. I can't believe I've found you."

Fly

Yelling for Joni, the officer muffles Maxine's cries with his hand, pulling her into him. Joni is raging.

"Now now, don't come near her, pretty boy, or I'll make sure all that dainty handywork of yours, is reversed. You did a good job. It'd be a shame to give you more work to do now, wouldn't it?"

Running for the exit like a stampede of elephants, people scream, opening the door, running down the stairs to the entrance. As the doors open and close, the distant sound of police sirens can be heard getting nearer.

Inside the club, those of us left listen to Joni's cries of terror, screaming at the officer with hatred.

"You bastard. I'll fucking kill you. Let her go. *Let her go!*"

Dragging Jayden to the side, checking to see if he's still alive, suddenly he's pushing himself up from the ground, horrified he can do anything after losing so much blood. No one has seen him, too transfixed on what is happening between Joni and the officer behind us. Holding his side, Jayden tells me to shh, bending to retrieve a knife from inside his sock. Shaking my head back and forth, he ignores me, running towards the officer, screaming, ramming the knife into the officer's neck as hard as he can.

Clink.

Still standing, the knife in the officer's hand drops to the floor as he looks ahead at nothing. Maxine is suddenly released from his hold, punching him in the ribs from behind with her elbow before she runs to Joni's arms. Stumbling forward, the officer falls to his knees, stretching his hand towards Maxine who's watching in horror as his voice penetrates the air.

"I only wanted you ... one ... last ... time. My little ... bird."

Seconds later, landing on his own knife, he takes his last breath as Jayden kicks him hard from behind.

Thwack!

"That's for Maxine."

Whack.

"That's for me."

Thud.
"That's for everyone at Nordsworth Prison."
Thump.
"That's because I can, you fucking prick."

Falling to the ground beside the officer, Jayden doesn't move, groaning, calling for Maxine to come to his side. Feet as light as air run towards her brother, crouching down to him as Joni turns the officer's body over exposing his deformed face to the light. Melted skin fused together looks like candle wax has hardened on his face; two piercing cold blue eyes stare up to the ceiling, his creepy clown grin smiling for the last time. Crawling to his body, staring into his eyes with hate, Maxine spits on his face.

"Welcome to hell, you *monster*."

Calling for his sister, Maxine turns back to Jayden whose breathing is laboured. Crying, taking his hand, she begs him to stay alive.

"Don't die, brother. Please, don't die."

"Forgive me, Max. Please? I'm so sorry. I'm so sorry for everything."

Reaching into his trouser pocket, he places something in Maxine's hand. Staring at it, crying, she tells him to hang on as he puts his hand on her lips.

"I'm so sorry, my sister. Joni. Look after her. Look after her for me, please? I love you so much, Maxine. I always have, you know that."

There's not even a hush as Jayden's eyes close and both Maxine and I scream *"no"* in unison as police officers run through the door.

Wellington has never seen anything like it before. It turns out the officer was wanted for a string of assaults on a number of strippers, and now, because Maxine is able to take the police to the place she was attacked, he is officially accused for the murder of a woman whose body they find very close to where she was attacked. It turns

Fly

out she's been missing for a number of years, her family finally able to put her to rest.

Ricki was in so much shock, he had to close the club for a couple of weeks while police investigations were carried out, and frightened the club would be snubbed by people and he'd have to close it down, he was absolutely delighted the exact opposite happened when DevO's finally reopened.

It proved so popular; people had to queue up around the corner to get in. They wanted to have their photo taken on the spot where the officer died, but Ricki put a stop to that, saying it wasn't a freak show.

Joni became a local celebrity, too, drawing more people than ever to the place. He drew the line at people taking his photo, though. There were some things he just wouldn't do. Maxine thought it was hilarious. He didn't.

A week later, recovering from an operation on a severed lung, Jayden sits up, lucky to be alive. Arrested for the murder of the officer, he will stand trial when he's fit enough. In the meantime, a police officer has been put on duty outside his hospital door twenty four hours a day to make sure he doesn't escape. The doctor on duty the night he was bought to hospital, and who later performed his surgery, told Maxine he was one lucky man. If the knife had been even one millimetre to the right, Jayden would not have made it.

Sitting up, bruised and sore with needles stuck everywhere, Jayden waits to see Maxine, who still hasn't told him about Lola, or me.

Waiting impatiently outside Jayden's room, Joni, Lola, Sharon, and myself listen as Maxine talks to him. Anxious to see how he'll react, we don't have to wait too long. Opening his box, he stops, holding up his hand for Maxine to stop. She's told him.

"*You and Lola are what? You're lying!* It can't be true, Max. They're having you on. Lola can't be your sister."

Listening outside the door, which has been left open ever so slightly by Maxine, Jayden's voice is high, like he's in shock.

"*No!* It's not true. Max. Please tell me it's a joke. Please?"

Looking towards us for moral support, thankfully Jayden doesn't follow her eyes, breathing with relief as we see he is covering his own eyes while her words sink in.

"It's not a joke, Jayden. Mum left me a letter. You know the one you didn't open? It explains *everything*. You have to read it. You *have* to read it. You owe it to everyone you've hurt. You know you do. You have to ask for their forgiveness, Jayden. If you don't, this will be the last time you ever see me. I mean it. Jesse's been through hell with you. You're lucky she's not pressing charges for killing her cat. She's my cousin. Gail was mine and Lola's birth mother, and she was also Jesse's mum's older sister. Jesse didn't even know she had an auntie. You need to make it up to her more than anyone else. Oh, and by the way, you better go back to what used to be our house and ask our mother for forgiveness, too. I don't bloody care if you hated her, she didn't deserve what you did to her for all those years. None of us deserved it. You need to get help, you know that."

Hearing Jayden cry, it's like the old version of him never existed. Perhaps seeing his sister again has resurfaced memories he thought long forgotten. Or perhaps he can finally let the past go and start to live. Hugging each other, brother, and sister cry into each other's shoulder; Joni, Lola, Sharon, and myself look on in sympathy. Never in a million years did any of us think we would start to thaw, actually start to feel sorry for the one person we all hated so much. Patting Joni's shoulder and flicking my head towards Lola and Sharon, we all watch as Maxine wipes Jayden's eyes and starts to talk again.

"You also need to make things better with Lola and Joni if me and you are ever going to move on. If it weren't for Joni, I wouldn't be here. You know that. He's my saviour. I *love* him, so you have to find a way of being happy for me. We're going to get married, soon, so you better hurry up and get better if you want to be the best man, you hear?"

Fly

Watching them through the slit in the door, crying, holding each other tight, I want to hurt Jayden for what he did to me, to Samantha. I know people say that to forgive is to be free, but I'm not ready and don't know if I ever will be ready to forgive him. Or the pervert. I've forgiven others, but not them. God will understand.

My whole life my relationship with God has been strained. I've constantly asked Him over and over why things have happened in my life, and I've blamed Him, ignored Him, begged Him so many times to show me a sign, anything to make sense of what's happened. The fact that He's allowed Jayden and the pervert to live after all they've done, that *He's* forgiven them is something I'll never understand. What Jayden and the pervert did to me, to my Samantha, is something I will never get over. Seeing my beautiful cat killed by Jayden's hands is something I will never unsee.

Lola, social workers, foster parents, even my mother, I've forgiven. Jayden and the pervert, though? Hell will freeze over before I ever forgive them.

Looking at Jayden through the window, a weight suddenly lifts from me. The resentment, the anger, the hatred I've felt for him for so long doesn't feel so strong because I know he can't hurt me anymore. He can't hurt anyone I love anymore, and that comfort is all I need to go on. In that sense I'm free.

In that sense, I'm finally free.

Chapter Twenty-Four

If you cannot find peace within yourself, you will never find it anywhere else.

— Marvin Gaye

Walking back to The Orchard through the park, listening to Lola, Maxine, Sharon, and Joni chat about different things, I'm not paying any attention to their conversations, too distracted by the cicada's talking to each other, the gentle wind singing as the trees around me sway in time to their chirping. People walking past stop and admire the glorious colours of the flowers, smiling, smelling them as an aeroplane above interrupts the peace, cupping my eyes with my hand and watching with others who I know share in my want for it to go away. I can't help but think, is it going to England, my dream destination.

A child ahead of me suddenly screeches, possibly hungry, or maybe a bee or wasp has stung it. A scruffy blond, bearded hobo in a Kermit the Frog vest sleeps on his right side underneath a tree, instantly recognising him, upping my pace to get away from him, fast.

Fly

He has his right hand settled in between his legs, his left hand resting on his chest. He looks so weak. Beside him another scruffy, dark-haired man is on all fours exploring what is there. Setting up a camera to take a photo of himself, he lays provocatively on his side, smiling at the camera, making me wonder who he's taking the photograph for.

Far away cars drive to and fro, all the noises coming together like an orchestra of natural and man-made things. Someone behind me hums, adding to it as a tree in front of me sways almost in time with the humming, like it's dancing to their tune. The park is so green, lush, and colourful. Summer is here in all its glory.

Yellow, purple, white, pink, and red flowers adorn the pathway we're walking on, two lovers on a bench under a tree are almost invisible, talking, gazing into each other's eyes. Someone walks towards us in a bright-yellow dress, waving, smiling at us, not instantly recognising Celeste who is out for a stroll through the park with Matteo. Stopping and embracing me, I introduce her to Maxine and Joni while Lola looks on in a sulk, and Sharon smiles from the side. Promising to meet up soon for a coffee, we all watch them stroll off arm in arm, happy, in love, Lola scowls and blows a raspberry behind their back reminding me how immature she is.

Ignoring her, suddenly feeling tiny splatters of water hitting my skin, I think it's raining, looking up to the clear blue sky and back to the ground where sprinklers are feeding the grass. The coldness is welcome on such a warm day. Another plane interrupts the peace, and Lola and Sharon comment on how loud it is as Joni quickly kisses Maxine telling her he'll see her later before walking off towards town, waving to us as he crosses the road.

Watching them, I haven't concentrated on what they've been saying since leaving the hospital. It's like I've been inside my own bubble, floating in the air, or perhaps a cloud has picked me up and let me ride on it. The lightness I feel is unreal, the warmth inside my heart feels like a hand has wrapped itself around it and squeezed it tight. I don't know if it's real, but I swear I can feel a hand patting me on the back right now. It's like someone is trying to tell me everything is alright. I know it's Gail. Or Samantha. My heart has finally thawed, and somehow, I'm at peace with not only the world, but myself, too.

I'm finally free.

Sitting around my kitchen table back at The Orchard, I make a coffee for Sharon, Lola, and Maxine, smiling, listening to Sharon who's reminiscing about her life with Gail in the early days. Elbows entwined, Maxine and Lola squeeze each other tight, emotional to hear all the stories of their birth mother. I'm emotional, too. I would've loved to have been able to get to know my aunt that little bit more. I will always be grateful to her for finding me. I will always be grateful to God for leading me to her.

Removing the necklace from around my neck, kissing the centre, I look up to the heavens and close my eyes, silently letting Gail know it has finally been reunited with its rightful owner. Grabbing Maxine's coffee and asking her to hold out her hand, she looks on with curious eyes.

"In all the happenings of late, I forgot to give you this. Gail gave it to me the night before she died. She asked me to wear it until it was reunited with its rightful owner, which is you. It was the only thing that connected her to you. She'll be so happy that you have it. She'll be so happy you and Lola are together."

Taking it from my hand, telling her to look through the centre, my heart bursts with love when she squeals with delight at seeing The Lord's Prayer. I still can't believe she is Lola's twin. It's surreal. They are so different yet so alike. Her squeal is exactly the same as Lola's, and Sharon can't take anymore.

"You girls are too noisy for me. Maxine, you sound just like Lola! I've got things to do. I still can't believe you girls are all related. Gail would've been so happy, so proud."

Kissing us all on the head before she leaves, Maxine and Lola hug her in unison, squeezing her so tight she has to force them off.

Fly

They've become inseparable. Lola still hasn't told her parents about Gail, or Maxine, which she's freaking about. Her dad never did turn up the night we were going to confront Jayden. He told her there was an emergency at home, which is most definitely a lie. I think it's good he didn't come. It would've been too much for Lola to deal with.

Watching them compare necklaces, the contrast between the two is massive. Where Lola is blonde, Maxine is dark. Lola is as tall as a tree and Maxine is as dainty as a flower. Both, though, have the same beautiful oval-shaped face, and the most stunning almond-shaped eyes. Lola's are hazel, more like Gail's and Maxine's are the colour of the deep-blue ocean, obviously the same as their father's. If only we knew who he was. It would be so perfect.

Interrupting, telling them about a letter I found in one of Gail's books, their ears prick up, turning to me with excitement.

"A letter? You never told me about this, Jesse."

Lola's pissed. I can tell by the way her teeth are making a sucking noise over her bottom lip. She always does than when she's angry. Maxine, thankfully comes to the rescue.

"Go and get it, Jesse. Please. Read it out to us."

Finding the book and opening it, I jump when a photograph of a young Gail and a mystery man falls to the floor. Picking it up, they are looking lovingly into the camera. Could he be Lola and Maxine's father? He's so blonde, almost ethereal looking. He doesn't look anything like the two girls sitting in front of me. There's no resemblance whatsoever, deciding it can't be. Turning it over, the name Pascoe is on the back in Gail's handwriting. All it says is, 'my first love.'

Hand to heart, trembling, I give the picture to Lola and Maxine and open the letter, reading it out loud for the first time.

Chapter Twenty-Five
Maddie

Honesty is always the best policy.

— George Washington

7th March 1975 – Age Thirteen

My darling Abigail,

Mother's just told me we are leaving in an hour. I don't know where we are going, so this is probably my last chance of contacting you.

My heart is crying.

It's breaking in two and won't be whole again until we are together. However long that is, is anyone's guess. How am I ever going to live without you?

I will keep you safe, in my heart. I will think about you every single day for the rest of my life and

Fly

will always wonder what you're doing, who you are with, if you are happy.

God, I hope you are happy. That would be the best gift in the whole wide world, to hear that you are not only free, but happy, too.

By the time you read this I will be gone. One of our other uncles is coming to take us far away from here, so I don't have long to write this.

Don't worry, things haven't been as bad as you've probably expected. Mother has stopped me going to Uncle Louie's. Once he started touching his own grandchildren, that was enough for the family. He has finally been sent to jail, where he belongs. I hear that the inmates at Nordsworth Prison have heard he's a pervert and are taking turns with him. The guards, apparently, are all turning a blind eye.

God does work in mysterious ways.

Perhaps Mother feels a tiny bit of guilt. I don't know for sure, but I think she has found God again. I think He's finally thawed her heart. I hope so.

She doesn't tell me, but I know she misses you. I hear her crying most nights, praying for you. She asks God to protect you and keep you safe. Maybe losing you and finding out about Uncle Louie has helped her find her way back to the light. I cry most nights, too, but they are happy tears that you are away from all this. Thank God you are safe. If only I'd had one last chance to see you. My only thanking grace, is that I got to see you many times before we parted. I'm so happy you kept coming to see me. I will love you forever and ever for that.

Darling Abigail, I know you will be blaming yourself for not coming back and getting me, but I want you to know, I forgive you. I forgive you for everything. It was you who protected me and tried to keep me safe my whole life, and I don't know what I would've done growing up if you hadn't been there. You are, and always will be my rock, my darling older sister.

I will love you forever and ever and ever, and will miss you to the moon and back.

I've got my necklace, the one we received on our First Holy Communion. Do you remember? I wear it every day and look into the centre and pray to the Lord that you have taken yours. Please be wearing it, too. I don't know if we will ever be reunited, but if we aren't, please rest assured that God will bring us together again one day. I believe it, and so should you.

Until then, I love you more than words can say.
Goodbye,

Your loving sister,
Maddie xxxx

Chapter Twenty-Six
Jesse

Forgiveness is the final form of love.

— *Reinhold Niebuhr*

"She had another necklace. How nuts that your mum's out there somewhere wearing the same necklace, Jesse. I think it's sad. She wasn't all bad, you see. Something terrible must've happened to her when she was young. Uncle Louie was definitely to blame for making her like she is. The perverted bastard! He must've done terrible things to both your mum and Gail. He was a creep, just like the pervert who touched you up. Surely that's what changed her into the monster she is. She wasn't always bad, Jesse."

Staring at the letters on paper, they all mix together as the realisation of what Lola's saying is right. Something terrible must've happened to my mother. Her uncle was to blame for making her the monster she is today. But if that's the case, why did she then allow the same thing to happen to me? That's what I can't get my head around. I'd love to be able to talk to her, ask her why, but even if I did, I know she wouldn't tell me the truth. Knowing she had an equally abusive upbringing, should I follow my heart and try to forget all the terrible things she has said and done to me over the years. Is it the right thing to do, not only for me, but for Gail, too? They were sisters.

Squeezing my hand, Maxine smiles, hugging me tight.

"I know you've been through so much with your mother, and now Jayden, but please, try and forgive him. It wasn't easy growing up with parents like ours. From what I've heard about your mother, she was pretty much the same as our father, except for the God thing. If our father had found God he would've been a different person for sure. Jayden always had it much harder than me. Just from talking to him recently, I know he feels really sorry for everything he's put me, and you through. He's owned up to it all, and is even having therapy for it now. I would never have imagined he'd do that. *Ever!* I think finding me again, and finding out Lola is my twin, and that we're all cousins, has given him a reason to change. Something inside his soul has flipped. It sounds nuts, but I think we've given his life meaning again, and I know you'll understand when I say the monster my mother and I, and you, lived with all those years, is gone. Something's happened. God, or maybe a sense of peace has come to him. He's not even worried about going to jail. The lawyers dealing with his case are saying he probably won't even get charged for murder because he was protecting me. It's a miracle. I know it's hard, but do you think you could try and build a friendship with him? Try and forgive him?"

Looking into Maxine's eyes, my heart just can't forget what he did. If I'm honest, I'm still taking in Gail's letter, turning the page over and over, trying to make sense of it all. Squeezing her hand, smiling into her anxious eyes, I softly answer her.

"I don't know, Max. It's a hard one. After what he did to me, and especially to Samantha. She was my life. I loved her so much and miss her every day. The pain is still here, right inside my heart, and it's not budging."

Pointing to my heart, I hold it as if in pain.

"I'll never forget what he did to Samantha. As for being friends? I don't know. I'm not quite there, yet and don't know if I'll ever be. I'll always be here for you, though, Maxine. Always."

Maxine's smile is hopeful, which I suppose is something for her. So much energy has been wasted over the years, I don't know if I have any more to give where Jayden's concerned. I want to focus on the good people in my life, now, not the ones who've ruined it.

Leaving Lola and Maxine to chat about the photo, I put the letter back in its envelope and hear a knock at the door. Opening it to nothing, looking around, there's a faint squeak at my feet, looking down and seeing a big brown box on the doorstep. Wrapped around it is a pink ribbon, and an envelope attached to it has writing, 'open me.'

Not overly heavy, I quickly take it inside and place it on the table where we all look at it, watching as something inside it moves.

"OMG, open it, Jesse. There's something moving inside."

Lola's excited, and Maxine is just looking frightened.

"What the hell is it? Go on, Jesse. Open it before I pee my pants."

Following Lola's eyes, slowly unwrapping the ribbon, I open the box and look inside, gasping, not believing my eyes.

"No way!"

My heart bursts into tears.

A kitten, the same colour as Samantha, meows up at me, picking it up and cuddling it. Crying, I look underneath to see it's a girl and suddenly all the memories of Samantha come flooding back. Attached to the box is a note.

She will never replace Samantha, but I know you will love her. You deserve to be happy. J x'

Reading the note, both Lola and Maxine ask in unison.

"Jayden?"

Chapter Twenty-Seven

A friend forgives quicker than an enemy, and family forgives quicker than a friend.

— *Amit Kalantri*

Two weeks later, walking towards DevO's on a Wednesday night, Lola, Maxine, and I drag a very nervous Tiffany to the entrance, telling her everything will be fine.

After hearing her story one drunken night, we spent hours convincing her to try and mend bridges with Joni. Maxine especially wants the reunion, saying it will be the best wedding present ever if she is there. Convincing Tiffany to come to the club was harder than walking on water. Roy laughed at us when we rang and asked for advice.

"Why do you think I rent her a place of her own? Even I know how impossible it would be if we lived together. I like my own space. Good luck getting her to do what you want. Stubborn is Tiffany's middle name."

I don't think any of us were quite prepared for how stubborn

Fly

she'd be but, by some miracle, we got her to agree. Though now that she's about to do it I think she's got cold feet.

This will be the first time she's talked to Joni in years, so I understand why she's so anxious.

Linking arms, feeling her trembling, I squeeze her hand and look into her eyes, nodding, trying to reassure her that all will be good.

In the meantime Lola and Maxine go and get Joni, giving us a quick kiss before they walk towards the entrance of the club arm in arm, looking back and blowing us a kiss again as they enter.

Joni's happy to see them, grinning from ear to ear when they plant a kiss on either side of his cheek. They look so happy twirling on each of his arms, like ballerinas on the stage.

Maxine takes Joni aside, seeing her tell Lola to shh with her finger, taking his arm and pointing to something outside. His worried eyes follow her, quickly changing to anger as he stops, angrily talking and pointing to where I and a very anxious Tiffany stands.

Twiddling her thumbs like she has something stuck to them, Tiffany looks at me sideways, noticing the sweat beginning to build on her forehead. I'm hoping she's not thinking of doing a runner. Whispering to me in a voice far from confident, she is fearful, like a child going into confession for the first time not knowing what to say.

"I don't know if I can do this, Jesse. What if he doesn't want to see me? I'll look like a fool. Look at him. His face isn't friendly at all. Why did I let you girls talk me into this?"

Turning to run, I grab her arm, squeezing it tight, looking straight into her eyes.

"Tiffany, if you don't do this now, you never will. Remember what they say, if you don't try, then you've already failed. Just see what he says. At least you can say you tried. C'mon, you've come this far. Don't fall at the last hurdle. You can do this."

Leading her to where Joni and Maxine stand, brother and sister eyeball each other as traffic passes. People on the street look on, sure they expect something is going to happen, one girlfriend telling her boyfriend to shut up and look away. Maxine flicks her head towards me and I gently push Tiffany forward, making her stumble on her heels, which makes Joni rush forward to catch her. Hand in hand, their eyes connect, two frightened children unsure how to act. I can't breathe watching the exchange. Tiffany speaks first.

"H-h-hey brother. It's me. Your big sis. Remember? I don't want to fight or be strangers anymore. Do you think we could start over? Forget about what's happened and be happy again? I've stood outside and watched you for years just to get a glimpse of you. You know I love you more than life. Don't you?"

Looking straight into her face, still holding her hands, Joni's look is stern, like he wants to turn her around and make her leave, but all of a sudden, his eyes become soft and tears cascade down both cheeks, like a waterfall finding the sea.

"Of course I can, my *sister*. Forgive me, please. I'm so sorry for everything. You know I love you and only want you to be happy. I've been foolish. A stupid fool. Au lomani iko, ganequ."

"I love you too, my brother. I'm so happy. Please, let's never be apart again."

Hugging for what seems minutes, they break apart, wiping each other's tears, patting each other down. Linking arms, Joni proudly leads Tiffany inside DevO's, stopping to ask Brendan, the guy who's been covering him on the door, to give him another half an hour. My heart is jumping for joy as I link arms with Maxine and Lola, the three of us following Joni and Tiffany up the steps and into the club.

Waiting inside is Roy, anxious to see if brother and sister are reunited. Welling up when they walk through the door arm in arm, Joni presents Tiffany to him, taking his hand in his.

"Welcome to the family, brother. I can't thank you enough for taking care of my sister for all these years. I and our family owe you so much."

Hugging him, there are tears all round as Ricki turns from what he's doing and asks what is happening. Patting his cheeks, winking, and taking his arm, Lola answers Ricki, arching her eyebrow at him.

Fly

"Oh, you know, Ricki. Just another typical Wednesday night at DevO's."

Cyndy, Ricki's girlfriend, stands beside him glaring at Lola, who I think is not going to let anything spoil our night.

"Cyndy, FYI, I don't *want* Ricki. I'm really not interested in old men."

Looking at him, Lola kisses both his cheeks.

"You know I love you, Ricki, but you're old enough to be my *father*. I really don't want to fight anymore with Cyndy, so could you please just stop flirting with anything that moves and give the poor girl a break?"

Extending her hand to Cyndy, Lola says, "truce?" Waiting for her to take her hand, Cyndy shakes it, smiling at Lola, hugging her, leaving Ricki in shock as we follow the others to our reserved table.

Lola's shoulders are tight, squeezing them from behind, whispering softly in her ear.

"Miracles really do happen if you wait long enough. I'm proud of you, Lola."

Squeezing my hand, she turns giving me a thumbs up to signal she likes the song Greg is playing, watching him bopping about in his booth. Spotting us as we give him the thumbs up, we dance along with him to 'Certain Things are Likely' by Kissing the Pink, shocked that Lola even knows the song.

Winking at me, raising her eyebrows, she comes just close enough for me to hear, waving at Ramona who's just walked in.

"You know, I quite like a little bit of kissing the pink."

Laughing, watching her run to Ramona and kiss her, I'm undecided whether I'm dreaming. I've always had an inkling Lola might like girls, but now that it's confirmed, I don't know what to think.

Luring Joni up for a dance, Maxine grabs Tiffany and Roy to join them and I quickly go and say hi to Greg, who's taking a break in his booth. Asking for a song I haven't heard for ages; he's setting it up when Lola sashays up with Ramona. His look says it all. He's definitely not happy to see her, and Lola lets rip.

"For fuck's sake, Greg. I'm bloody sick of the way you look at me. What the fuck have I ever done to you to make you hate me like this. I don't even know you. What the hell is your problem?"

Eyes bulging out of his head, swearing I see steam coming out of his ears, his nostrils are fully flared and his back is stiff, like a dog with its hackles up. I don't think I've ever seen him look this angry.

"I'll tell you what my problem is, *Zoe Freeman!* Don't you recognise the boy you used to terrorise at school? Gregory? Well, he's all grown up now, and he ain't gonna put up with you, or your crap any longer. *You hear.* You may have been able to boss everyone around back then, and you may be able to boss everyone now, but you're *not* going to boss me around anymore. *Never again!*"

Mouths agape; Lola and I stare up at him, unblinking, confused, in shock. It can't be Gregory, the kid who used to cause merry havoc at school for however many years. Surely, one of us would've recognised the geeky walk, the front teeth, the wild, curly, black hair? Where are his glasses? They were so huge. It can't be him. Why didn't I click it was him?

Suddenly Lola's shaking, ready to explode; Ramona doesn't stand a chance of stopping her.

"Are you serious? *You're Gregory?* The geek who always used to pee in the reading corner. You're the geek who always used to get into trouble with the teachers? It doesn't even look like you. Where are your glasses? You're bloody lying. *You're lying!*"

"*No,* I'm not, you snooty bitch. I don't even know why Jesse is still your friend. I've wanted to tell her so many times who I am."

Looking towards Ramona, Greg points to Lola, shaking his head at her.

"If I were you, I'd be running for the hills. She'll use you and hurt you like she did to so many kids at school. She was such a horrible bitch. *A bully!* Run while you can."

Grabbing his finger, Lola's ready to kill, but Ramona stops her, pushing her to the side as she continues screaming over her shoulder at him.

Fly

"Why didn't you say something when we first met then, eh? Why have you waited until now to tell me? *You dick!*"

Headphones on, Greg starts mixing the next song, his left index finger telling her to wait. As *'People are People'* starts playing, Lola stands, hands on hips, her eyes bulging, like a frog that's been squeezed. This is not going to end well. Removing his headphones, shaking his head, and pointing his finger at Lola, Ramona and I just roll our eyes and wait.

"I didn't tell you because I thought you'd figure it out. You haven't changed one little bit. You're still a stuck-up little princess. I hated you so much at school. You made my life a bloody misery. You and all your little followers made mine and Jesse's life a misery. I couldn't believe she started hanging around with you. You know I had to move schools because of *you*. You and your gang of followers. Look at you now, eh? Where are they all. No one but Jesse left. Not so tough now, are you."

I don't want tonight to go down this route, urging Lola to say sorry, but she's having none of it. Ramona comes to the rescue, taking Lola aside, softly talking to her until she nods, looks over at Greg and walks back. Breathing in deep, cracking her neck muscles, she starts speaking through gritted teeth.

"Love the choice of song, you dick! Anyway, I'm sorry. I know I was a right little bitch back then to you, and Jesse, but I don't know why I did the things I did. Back then I was only a kid, remember? I was trying to fit in, too. I mean, did you even know my mother? I know that's no excuse, but please, let me make it up to you. I don't know what else to say. Hit me if you want. I deserve it. Just don't go anywhere near my face. Go on, I deserve it."

Closing her eyes, Lola waits for Greg to hit her. Eyeballing her, looking at Ramona and I until he bursts into laughter, Lola opens her eyes and starts laughing, too.

"What the hell? Why would I hit you? I don't want to hurt you. I just wanted to hear you say sorry and mean it."

Laughing along, Lola comes clean, telling Greg and I that her and Ramona are going steady. Like we didn't guess.

Happier and more relaxed than I've ever seen her, she's not so uptight, which can't be said for the usual flock of men she attracts. They're hanging around looking at her and Ramona with a mixture of lust and confusion. Arms in the air, nodding to each other, I don't think they know what to do. I've got to give it to Lola. She's looking at them like she couldn't give a rat's arse about any of them, happy to show Ramona off to the world. Grabbing Greg and hugging him, he's stiff but soon backs down and hugs her back. I don't think he wants to fight anymore, and I'm sure he doesn't want to see her unhappy, either, watching as she asks Ramona to come stand by her. Taking her hand in hers, smiling and kissing her lightly on the lips, Lola looks into Ramona's eyes with what looks like love, and turning to Greg and I, her face and voice are soft.

"I suppose for all these years I was battling against something that was always meant to be. I always knew I was bi, but didn't want to admit it. Please, forgive me. I'm truly sorry, Greg, and Jesse."

Hugging again, I can't believe that Lola and Greg, sworn enemies, are friends at last. I'm also in shock hearing her say sorry to me. She's another person, someone I always knew was in there, wishing she'd had the courage to do this when we were younger. Everyone's lives at school would've been so much happier. Poor Mrs Glennis wouldn't have had to put up with years of torture from any of us. I wonder what she's doing now. I hope she's happy.

Someone waves at Lola from the dancefloor, an old man who I haven't seen before. Nudging her in the ribs to make her see, she squeals with delight, running down to greet him. Seeing her hug and take him by the hand, she brings him up to where we stand. Arm in arm, I'm guessing this is Alan, her dad.

"Jesse, Ramona, Greg, I want you to meet my dad, Alan. Dad, this is Jesse, my best friend, Greg the DJ, and this is Ramona - my girlfriend."

Fly

Kissing him on the cheek, it's surreal to finally be meeting him. It's taken so long.

Short and a little rounder than I thought he'd be, he's dressed in blue pressed jeans and a white collared shirt with a mustard waistcoat covered in intricate embroidered flowers. The long, western-style, tasselled, brown jacket and cowboy boots make him look like he's stepped straight off a western movie. Short dark hair that's definitely been dyed, his stubble isn't the same colour, giving away his age. Asking us politely to wait while he and Lola talk privately, they walk off while Ramona and I watch everyone dancing, jumping up for joy at the next song. *'Drop Dead Gorgeous'* by *Republica* is one of my favourites, blowing Greg a kiss because he knows how much I love Saffron.

Five minutes later, Lola is back with Alan. I don't know if she's told him about Maxine, but I suppose if she hasn't it can wait one more day. I think there's only so much a parent can take for one night. Not surprised her mother hasn't come, that would've been way too much to expect.

Asking Lola a few minutes later where her mother is, she tells me that her parents have separated, and says her dad will tell her why tomorrow.

"Maybe I wasn't wrong after all, Jesse. Don't ever discount your gut. It always lets you know. I'm happy for him. I'm happy he's finally free and will be able to be the person he wants to be. I know how that feels."

Offering to buy us all a drink, Alan walks to the bar and I volunteer to tag along to help. Squeezing Lola's arm before I go, I'm happy she's finally got some answers. I would never have dreamed that conversation we had months back would have actually turned into reality. Not for one minute would I have thought her dad was gay, but I wouldn't have thought Lola was gay either. It just goes to show how little we really know people. Lola and her father can now be the people they want to be freely without the wrath of her mother threatening them in any way. That in itself must be a great weight off both their shoulders.

Walking to the bar with Alan, it's nice to finally be able to chat to him. Jayden's talking to Maxine who's handing him something from her pocket. Eavesdropping, I just hear what she's saying.

"Remember you gave me this out of your pocket the night we were reunited. Now that you're not going to jail I can give it back to you. I've always loved these lighters. I just wish I still had mine."

Smiling at her, Jayden tells her to keep it, kissing her hand, looking at her with such love, it's hard to think he's the same man who beat me up for so long. Kissing him goodbye, Maxine passes us, waving as Alan stops in mid walk and stares at Jayden like he's seen a ghost.

"Jimmy? Jimmy? Is it you?"

Staring at Jayden with wide eyes, they are glazed over, and it looks like he's going to cry. Why? Patting his arm, making sure he's alright, I'm confused.

"No, his name is Jayden, but his dad was called James. Did you know him?"

Patting down his hair, smiling at me awkwardly as he pulls his waistcoat down, Alan nervously walks forward.

"Oh, it must be someone else. Jimmy was someone I knew a long time ago. He used to remind me of a young Warren Beatty. You wouldn't know him; it was probably long before your time. God, it was like looking at him again. It just spooked me a bit. C'mon, let's get those drinks, they'll be wondering where we've got to."

Smiling at him, I don't know if I have the heart to tell Lola. It'd kill her to know that Jayden's father might be the 'Jimmy' her father knew. Gail also knew a Jimmy. Was that him, too? If it was, then he could possibly be Lola's and Maxine's real father, which would make Jayden, Lola, and Maxine full blood siblings.

I'm not even putting it out to the universe.

Walking back with the drinks, Greg starts playing a song I love, seeing Celeste and Matteo waving at us from the dance floor. She

Fly

said she was coming but I never thought she'd turn up. Placing the drinks on the table and dragging Lola, Ramona, Maxine, and Joni to the dance floor, Alan comes down at the same time I'm waving at Tiffany, Roy, and now, Sharon, who amazingly has come. Waving at us from the door, Sharon drags Ricki and Cyndy to come join us as '*Freedom,*' by *George Michael* starts to play.

It's never sounded so good.

Grinning from ear to ear, thumbs up in the air, I, and everyone else, dance with abandon, singing along, grabbing each other, happy that nothing or anyone can hurt us anymore.

Jayden, who's watching from the bar, smiles lovingly at Maxine and Joni. Who would've thought that he and Joni would ever have called a truce. I think Jayden knows that without him, Maxine wouldn't be here, reunited with him, together, happy again. I'm sure he's sorry for everything that's happened between his sister, and me. I just hope he's as sorry for everything else that's happened in his life, especially with his mother. Only he knows what really happened to her. Only he can resolve it. For now, there's still so much none of us know. I'm not sure any of us really wants to. That might open up another can of worms and God knows we've already had enough of those.

Dancing, singing, happy, we all link arms, moving backwards and forwards, watching as Greg bounces around in his booth and waves at us while he changes the lights above to lasers. Mixing the next song, unlinking arms, jumping up and down to the opening riffs of '*Two of Hearts*' by *Staci Q*, I give him a massive thumbs up.

It's taken some time, but finally, I feel free. Finally, I have the family I want.

There's no mother, no pervert to hurt me anymore, hearing from one of the girls at The Orchard that the pervert was arrested for solicitation. One of the cops told her.

Apparently, Kevin is having lots of fun in Nordsworth Prison with a lunatic called Kurt. I hope it's the same Kurt from my past. He made my time at the foster home hell. Anton was lovely, though. I hope he's happy.

Someone suddenly squeals behind me, turning to see Ava and Anton. How in the hell has this just happened?

Hugging me tight, she tells me Jayden told her about me after Maxine told him I'd been fostered by her. Anton still looks the same, a little older for sure, but his eyes are still as kind as ever. Telling me Kurt is in prison, I raise my eyes to the ceiling silently thanking God, who I think has totally outdone himself. Asking about my mother, I let Ava know that she passed away from cirrhosis of the liver a while back. My steps are a hell of a lot lighter knowing I will never have to worry about bumping into her again, but I don't tell Ava that.

After my mother died I was sad, not for her, but more for a childhood lost. I would've loved to have had a normal life with a normal mother. I suppose it was never meant to be. I've forgiven her, but I'll never forget what she put me through. It's made me who I am today, so there's always something good that comes out of something bad. She left me some money, which I straight away donated to a domestic violence shelter. I would never have taken it. It's helped a lot of people. I felt she needed to do that to redeem herself. I can only hope that she and my aunt Gail are reunited, happy again. The thought of Gail being with her beloved sister, regardless of who she is, makes my heart sing.

Jumping, thumbs in the air, looking around to all the people I love, we all sing to the chorus of *'Two of Hearts,'* Lola and Ramona gesturing to each other, making hearts with their hands; Joni and Maxine dancing hand in hand, Ricki twirling Cyndy around with his right arm; Celeste and Matteo embracing, looking into each other's eyes with love. Ava and Anton are trying to pretend they even know the song, which cracks me up. Even Sharon and Alan are trying to guess the words, stifling a laugh as someone taps me lightly on the shoulder.

As Greg abruptly changes the song again, I recognise the opening riffs, smiling up at him as he points to whoever is behind me. Twirling

Fly

around to see who it is, I'm frozen, standing on the dancefloor like a statue as *Rick Springfield* sings '*Jesse's Girl.*' It can't be. I thought I'd never see him again, especially after the last time we'd been together.

Sashaying over with Ramona, Lola winks up at him, pushing me forward. What the hell? Cheeks on fire, looking up into a face I thought was long gone, I can't stop the little stars escaping from every part of my body. It has to be a dream?

"Hey, Jesse. How are you? I hope you like the song. I asked Greg to play it. I hope you liked my present, too? I bumped into Lola the other week and she told me about your cat. I'm sorry. I know you loved her, which is why I bought you another one just like her. I bet you didn't guess it was from me?"

"Dimples?"

The End

Acknowledgments

Finishing the final book of the series was like letting go of my baby. I've not known anything else for the last nine years and can't quite believe I'm done. I couldn't have done it without the support of my family.

My partner, Andy, has supported me throughout, and even though I know the genre of my books isn't his usual, he's still read them. From my heart to yours, thank you for everything you do, for being the calm to my storm when needed, and for always believing in me.

For Charley, my son, who gave me his permission to use his brand name and model one of the characters in book 2 after himself, you make me so proud every single day. Your support and love is all a mum could want. Thank you my heart. The world would be a much duller place without you.

For Cameron, my daughter, who is most probably the most patient person on this Earth. You listened, gave me a ton of advice, and supported me throughout the whole journey from start to end. You also designed all the brilliant covers for the series which only shows how creative and beautiful you are. Thank you my heart.

For Stephen, my stepson. You listened even when I knew you didn't want to. You bought my books and told your friends all about them, which I love you for. Thank you for everything and for being a beautiful person.

For Max, my stepson. Thank you for all the support and love throughout. I love you loads.

For Neil, my lovely father-in-law. Thank you for your support throughout the process and for being my biggest fan. You are the best father-in-law anyone could have.

For Sian Phillips, my lovely editor. You believed in me from the start, which gave me so much confidence in my writing. I've gained not only an editor, but a friend for life.

For Romie Nguyen, my typesetter. Thank you for your vision and for all your help and patience in making these books look so beautiful. Even though I asked you to redo the typeset a number of times, and revise when I thought I was done, you never complained and just did it which I will always be incredibly grateful for.

Lastly, thank you to all of you, the people who have bought my book. When I first started writing I was terrified no one would like my story or style of writing. I'm overwhelmed so many of you have liked them. I am forever grateful to each and every one of you. From my heart to yours, thank you.

About the Author

M.A. McNally writes page turning dark suspense in her fourth novel from the series *Broken*. In *Fly*, the characters she created in her first three novels will continue to have readers invested as they turn page after page. Part fact, part fiction, her stories are inspired by real life experiences and her early fascination with reading anything about true-life crime which started in her early teens, living in Wellington, New Zealand. Her earliest wish was to amaze the world with her rock star voice, but as that didn't work out, she finally let go of that dream and decided to focus on another. Writing. She's better at that - just.

Spending her days trying to inspire college students to love English language through writing, it's much harder than she thinks, but she's sure she's getting through to some of them. Her dream is to write full time, so she sits at the kitchen table early in the morning, and grabs an hour to write before work, clicking away on her keyboard while watching the sun say hello.

Currently living in Hampshire, England, she loves to sing (karaoke queen), go to gigs and the odd festival, but most of all she likes to catch up on the latest must see on television with her partner. Oh, and she loves all her kids.

Follow me!
On Instagram **@m.a.mcnally**
On Facebook & LinkedIn **Melissa A McNally**
On Tik Tok **M.A.McNally (@author.m.a.mcnally)**

Printed in Great Britain
by Amazon